Alison

Jane

Alison Sykes

Jane

Copyright © Alison Sykes 2024

All rights reserved. No part of this publication may be reproduced, stored in, or transmitted into any retrieval system, in any form, or by any means (electrical, mechanical, photocopying, recording or otherwise) without the prior written permission of the author.

This is a work of fiction. References to real people, events, practices, or localities are only intended to provide a sense of authenticity and are used fictitiously. Names, characters, businesses, places, events, and incidents are either the products of the author's imagination or used in a fictitious manner.

Disclaimer: Please note this book contains references to fictional accidents and medical procedures. These procedures should not be treated as medical advice. There are some scenes in *J a n e*, that some readers may find unsettling, related to the consequences and fallout of war.

First published in 2024 by Alison Sykes

Cover Courtesy of Canva

Dedicated to AWE

Chapter One
Mayfield Aerodrome, Lincolnshire
October 1942

An airfield in the autumn of war; a place of both dreams and ghosts.

A group of young women had assembled on the eastern most point of the perimeter, amongst the ancient earthworks and windswept fields of this part of Lincolnshire.

A whirlwind of dust and grass cuttings and they were grabbing for hats. Throttles of Spitfires opened above them: one, two, three, an unmistakable smell of oil and smoke as they lifted into the air.

Jane Harrison stood to the side of them, a sinking feeling in the pit of her stomach. What had she let herself in for?

Soon there was an overpowering growl - so loud that she was forced to cover her ears. Others took their chances, risking the deafening sound and grit in their eyes, until the last plane had taxied down the runway, the rhythmic beat of its engine fading into the distance; the scramble bell still ringing in their ears.

'Best of luck my friends!' came a shout from amongst them; the owner of the voice being a ruddy cheeked woman with the hearty complexion of someone who spent a great deal of time outdoors.

'And make sure you all damned well come back down again!'

The bell came to an abrupt stop.

'Amen to that!' agreed the woman standing to the side of her and who was now in the process of brushing dust from her sleeve.

The well-wisher nodded amiably. 'Phyllis Edwards,' she said offering a handshake, 'otherwise known as Phyll.'

'Jane Harrison,' responded her neighbour, now feeling a little more comfortable. 'Phyll' seemed approachable. Encouraged by the other woman's friendliness, she continued:

'That was quite a sight! I don't know whether to be alarmed or excited.'

'A bit of both I think. Looks like we've landed in the thick of it!'

'I suppose it was inevitable. Have you come far?'

'Yes, all the way from Cardiff. I came yesterday. It was too dangerous to try and drive in the blackout, though there are those that try.'

'Yes now that *is* foolish! It's bad enough during the day! I've come from Rye and the bus from the station took for ever!'

'Ah yes, the dreaded road blocks.'

Their conversation was interrupted by the appearance of another young woman, in the smartest of scarlet red hats.

She appeared to be the last to join the group as it continued to mix and mingle. They huddled together, unsure of what the day would bring; a few of them worrying about their cases which had been unceremoniously dumped in the guardroom, under orders from the receiving sergeant.

A flurry of activity and a uniformed officer emerged from a door in the building beside them. The group, uncertain of how to present themselves, stood silently awaiting instruction. The officer nodded to the assembled group and counted seven quickly. *Most satisfactory* she thought to herself. *No last minute drop outs!*

She was about to start proceedings when again there was the earth shattering sound of the scramble bell and a group of young men came hurtling out of a truck, driven at break neck speed towards a row of waiting spitfires. Within minutes they were strapped in and ready for take-off.

'Amongst the action already! Looks like we've picked a day for it.' The voice, crystal clear and confidant came from the woman in the scarlet hat.

Phyllis Edwards raised an eyebrow. 'More like we've been thrown in the deep end my friend!'

***

'Expect the unexpected,' announced the Commander, turning back to the business in hand. Five minutes of introductions and then the alarm goes off. This was something the recruits would have to get used to.

'I'll start again,' she coughed and cleared her throat. 'Welcome to Mayfield, your first day - and to the Air Transport Auxiliary. You're joining at a critical stage and for this you are much appreciated. There's an urgent need to free up our pilots from any other duty other than combat and that's where you will come in and why the ATA is so important.'

Jane Harrison felt a tingle in the back of her neck. She'd made it. They had all made it. A group of women, all with one thing in common: a passion to fly.

'We need you. It's as simple as that,' the officer continued. 'Your country needs you. The ATA will allow the RAF to concentrate on air defence. The Blitz may be over, but the Luftwaffe's now turning its attention to the Atlantic; so there's no let-up in the Battle in the Air I'm afraid.'

There was a nodding of heads. They had read enough to be aware of how things were hotting up for the Navy, battling to protect the convoys from the onslaught of U-boats.

'We have a significant shortage of pilots, wireless operators and gunners. Getting crews out to operational command is a priority. Training courses are down from eight to four weeks.'

Jane raised her eyebrows and swallowed hard. *That's why we're losing so many pilots,* she thought.

The woman in the scarlet hat raised a hand.

'Yes, Cadet?'

Her crystal-clear vowels clipped every word.

'When will training start Ma'am?'

'Good question and nice to see you're keen to get going. It begins tomorrow, first thing. You'll get the info later.'

The woman nodded, seemingly satisfied. She tucked a purse under her arm and patted down her hair. Golden waves were teased into the hat, which had a little netting over the forehead. She towered above the other girls. *She's like an Olympic Sprinter*, thought Jane, taking an unobtrusive glance at the line of her back and unconsciously holding her own head a little higher.

To the casual observer, the assembled group, may well have appeared an eclectic bunch. For a start, they clearly had widely differing views on what constituted the 'sensible attire' as requested be worn on the day. Bowes-Hudson and Maria Pérez wore the sharpest and closest fitting attire; V's being a triumph in body hugging tailoring. Edwards, Miller and Harrison all wore theirs loose, whist Johnston wore hers in an ill-fitting two piece. Lastly, there was Hattie Sykes, whose suit was eclipsed by a shimmering silk square, and with which she whipped out with a flourish to dab the grit from her eye.

The Commander looked at her watch. *Must get a move on. Aircraft to inspect and admin to sign off, she thought.* 'Training **will** be demanding, but you've been selected based on past competencies and I have every faith in you.' She turned and looked about. 'Now where's Sergeant Sanders? SERGEANT SANDERS!?'

A WAAF, in dirty overalls, came running out of a nearby Nissen Hut and skidded to attention.

'Sorry Ma'am.' She caught a breath; her dusty boots and oily hands, indicating that she'd only recently been plucked from the hangar floor.

Sanders will give you a tour and then your ground instructor, Captain Hadley will fill you in with the rest later.'

'Where to first Ma'am?' the WAAF asked, regaining her composure.

'Try Hangar 3. Always a lot going on there and see if you can sort out some tea. The canteen may have a few spare ounces if you're short.'

'Ma'am.'

The Commander stood to attention. 'Well, all that's left for me to say is, the *best of luck* Ferry Pool 6a.'

'Thank you, Ma'am,' the group replied with varying levels of confidence.

A car rolled up and a Corporal, with gleaming boots, opened the door on the passenger side.

The Commander saluted and then she was gone, wheels bouncing along the perimeter track and up towards the Guard Room.

The WAAF nodded towards the group. 'This way please! With any luck we'll catch a ride along the way.'

The group set off. Blasts of cold air were sweeping across the fields, barely broken by the artificial hedging erected to disguise the edges of the aerodrome. Phyllis Edwards rubbed her hands 'Flipping heck! It's cold. My hands can't feel a thing!'

'Not half as cold as we'll be in an open cockpit!' Brenda Sykes was glad she had worn two pairs of her thickest tights, even if they were hellishly itchy.

'Then I'll make sure I'm wearing very many socks!' Maria Pérez was chilled to the bone. 'It's so cold in your country!'

'Swops for the Med darling!' relied the woman in the scarlet hat. 'By the way,' she said stopping and fixing her blue eyes fixed on the horizon. 'Is that a truck I can see?'

The WAAF waved as it approached, its headlights dipping and flashing as it came to a stop on its large fat wheels.

A corporal leaned out of the window. He nodded towards the group.

'Afternoon, Corporal. Hanger 3 if you will.'

'Certainly, Ma'am. Backs open!'

The group climbed in, edging themselves along benches under the tarpaulin.

'All in!' The WAAF banged on the side of the truck as the driver spun the wheels. *Oh, for goodness sake! Just slow down!* Suddenly she felt cranky, exhausted. It had been a long night with numerous repairs.

The driver was oblivious and picked up speed. Verona Bowes Hudson or 'V' as she was known to friends was rather enjoying it. Speed was always exciting in her book. She smiled and held onto her hat. 'Someone's got his skates on!'

Jane nodded, looking out from the back and into the sky behind them. 'Talking of skates, I can't believe how quickly the squadron scrambled.'

'Pretty slick aren't they, two minutes tops,' nodded the sergeant. 'Spits have a long prop so you have to be careful not to push the stick too far on take-off or you could...'

'Risk a somersault?' V interjected.

'Right Ma'am.'

Phyllis Edwards held onto the side of the clanking truck, her thoughts elsewhere. The Scramble had unnerved her; this is what her Eddie would be doing day and night at Kenley. 'I have a question Sergeant.'

'Fire away!'

'How many of those Spits are likely to return?'

'It depends.' The WAAF grabbed a strap as the truck took a sharp turn. 'If it's been a hell of a raid, then maybe only half of them, if it's a good one then….'

'Change the subject old girl.' V rolled her eyes in the direction of Edwards and then with a smile added, 'a better question might be to ask what's the food's like here!'

The group laughed.

Phyllis Edwards smiled begrudgingly. 'Ok. You've got me there.'

The WAAF grinned. 'Not bad at all!' she said. 'I'd give the rice pudding a miss though!' The truck came to a screeching halt. They had arrived at a large building, camouflaged by greenery and a canopy of trees.

'Here we are!' shouted the driver. 'Hangar 3-door to door!'

'Thanks Corporal!' The WAAF jumped down pulling the ramp onto the grass, 'and get some oil for those brakes!'

'Ma'am.'

'Flipping racket! They probably heard that all the way to Munich!'

'Bloody cheek, more like,' the Corporal grumbled, as he started up the engine and slipped the handbrake off.

Chapter Two

The Bellman hangar in the northwest corner of the aerodrome had been damaged by heavy snowfall the winter before. Now, a new steel frame provided not only protection from the elements, but also an amplification of sound.

'Wow! The whole nine yards!' V nodded approvingly, her voice echoing in the vast chamber.

They were almost speechless. It appeared to be full of aircraft in all stages of repair; most of which, the group had not heard of or seen before.

'Damn it! You've got a fuselage up there! Hattie Sykes mopped her brow. The coke braziers were burning away. 'How on earth did you manage to winch it up?'

'Magic isn't it! Follow me, have a gander, but don't touch A THING!' The Seargeant waved them through.

Jane Harrison felt a knot in her stomach. It had been a bad night, anticipation causing restless sleep and fitful dreams. She felt wrung out. Only fifteen hours of dual control training to solo flight had brought her to this point.

Perhaps she just felt relieved.

For a moment, she thought of her father. What would he say if he could see he now? She was sure he would be proud. She had wanted to fly just like him and now here she was. She felt a lump in her throat. This was happening a lot lately. Little things would remind her of him; the smell of oil in the hangers, the heart thumping sound of a plane overhead, even the smell of floor polish in the Mess.

She steadied herself and took a deep breath. Joining the ATA had been important for two reasons; firstly, to make a contribution, using the skills she had and secondly, to fulfil a personal mission. It would be a chance to make contacts, to gather intelligence, to have her ears to the ground.

She remembered back to the news of her father's disappearance; coming as it did one Friday afternoon. She had been knee deep in hay, feeding the horses stabled at the Vets. The apprentice had been called up and he was shorthanded. She had offered her service and helped sooth the animals that were restless and nervy. The horses were particularly agitated. Anti-aircraft guns and the drone of planes had harnessed their natural need to bolt. Their pent-up energy could be seen in every twitch of their coats.

She was picking out hooves on the day she heard the alarm in her mother's voice as she ran across the yard; her voice straining in agony to read the telegram:

Concerning Squadron Leader G. Harrison. Missing in action. Presumed dead.

Jane did not cry, for she simply did not believe it. She stood there with the horse knocking the bucket out of her hand and flatly refused to acknowledge the final sentence.

Shortly after, she had taken a job in her aunt's grocery shop in Rye. It had paid enough to help with food and bills, with a little left over for fortnightly flying lessons, during which she had studied every waking hour. Now, finally here she was, in the ATA and closer to an answer.

'Aircraft like a kaleidoscope!' A voice broke through her concentration. Phyll Edwards was standing next to her. 'Except they're not bright colours, they're shades of mud!'

Jane nodded. 'A palette of greens and browns. I'm ready to get going now, aren't you?'

'I'd jump in now if I had half the chance!'

'Count me in!' The woman in the elaborate hat came over to join them. 'Let's hope we're out solo by the end of the week.'

Phyll laughed. 'I expect it will be a bit longer than that lovely!'

The woman scowled a little. 'Only if we're not up to scratch surely.'

'V' Bowes Hudson was not known for her patience. Flying was in her blood and she was ready to get going straightaway. It was her brother's fault. He had taken her up to feel the wind in her face and the sun on her hair. *This is how you clean your goggles Verona*, he had said, showing her how to use a white silk scarf to polish them up. Her brother had been the only one who had used her full name, chosen by her parents who had been holidaying there. It had been both a curse and a blessing.

She reached inside her pocket. The scarf was still there - well just a square of it, torn and ripped and grubby like an old worn comforter. She took a breath and looked about, so many *different* fuselages glittering in the damp air. She would whizz through this training; in fact, she would only need the bare minimum.

All it would take was a few practice flights.

The WAAF patted the underbelly of a Harvard. 'Have a look around, ask as many questions as you like. We'll meet back in the Briefing Room. I'll have sorted out a cuppa by then!'

Chapter Three

V's patience was wearing thin. The clock was ticking and still no sign of the captain. The group had spent the rest of the afternoon orientating themselves around the aerodrome and her feet were killing her. Plus, there had been a freezing cold walk back to the Mess, with a ghost-grey fog drifting and creeping around its stone columns and sweeping steps.

Still, at least I know who my billeting companions are and Harrison and Edwards seemed decent sorts. The cottage was definitely preferable to being billeted with a family or holed up in a guest house, however small it was. V was an independent sort; a result of absentee parents and a succession of nannies. She was also prone to haughtiness - a quality that could rub others the wrong way.

She needed to be on her best behaviour tonight.

***

Captain Pops Hadley opened the door to Room 5. Excellent, everything was in place: maps, models and pilot's notes. She approached the lectern, dumped a briefcase on the floor and shuffled her notes.

She positioned herself, leaning heavily on the cane in her hand.

'At ease!'

She glanced at the women in the room. They looked a competent bunch, though the short one might not have made the grade a few months earlier. How on earth was she going to reach the rudder bars?

For a moment she sensed adrenaline in the room, the quiet murmur of competition, stiff new shoes and egos to match. She took a tin from her pocket, proceeding to light a cigarette. Her eyes slanted like green almonds against the curl of smoke.

***

Phyll's mind was elsewhere. She was preoccupied with the weather and had been clocking the conditions. *October fog. Flipping obstruction. God knows what sorties lay in front of Eddie tonight.*

How on earth had she got here, either flying or preparing to fly. Never in a million years did she believe that it would have been possible.

That was until she met 'Eddie' David Edwards.

She has been helping out in her grandfather's shop, nestled as it was, in a narrow street on the outskirts of Cardiff. He was on the scout for a ration of tea and a tin of peaches and was fresh off the farm with dirty boots and fingernails to match. He had ventured into the city, having been sent on an errand to pick up some spare parts from an engineering firm.

They hit it off straight away. His face was ruddy and gentle. There was a large smudge of oil on his left check beneath the 'smiliest' of eyes and when she handed him the peaches she asked him:

'Why does Popeye like canned artichokes as well as peaches?

'You got me there!' He grinned packing the purchases into his pockets.

'Because they both need Olive Oil of course!'

'Very good,' he nodded, laughing. 'Very, *very* good!'

'Here,' she said offering him a handkerchief and small mirror. 'Tractors are oily beasts.'

She grinned at him; her broad, strong, rosy cheeks looking a little amiss within the confines of the small, poky shop.

'Thanks,' he rubbed vigorously at his cheek. 'But, this oil is from a different engine. I'm helping to fix a small aircraft.'

'An aircraft? How's that going to herd sheep?'

He laughed. 'Well, that's another story!'

'Then come again and tell me about it.' Phyll couldn't believe she had just said that.

He smiled, scratching around in his jacket pocket. 'How much do I owe you?'

'4d in total. Have you had the peaches before?'

'Before?' he repeated, handing her the money and his ration book.

'Only one tin per year I'm afraid. Must be a special occasion.'

'It is! First test flight after repairs. Definitely special!'

She nodded, checked his book and handed it back; even in the gloomy light he could see how lovely she was.

'Are you free this weekend?'

She laughed. 'You're not shy at coming forwards are you!'

He nodded, shrugging his shoulders. 'War is looming again.'

There was no need to reply. She knew exactly what he meant. The last one seemed only a whisper away. Everything was different now; no one had time to wait for anything anymore.

She agreed and met him the following weekend at the gate of a large sheep farm amongst the hills at the back of the city. A small light-weight biplane was lying idle on a levelled field. There were banks of turf like an embankment around it and a small crowd had gathered.

He smiled broadly. 'It's an Avro Avian, in case you're wondering.'

She laughed. 'Now *why* wouldn't I know that!'

'Never doubted it!' In an impulse he offered his arm. 'Come and meet the team!'

Eddie and his two younger brothers farmed between them, having lost their father at an early age. They had grown up around engines and were used to mechanical 'tinkering,' as their mother liked to call it. The little wooden biplane had come their way via a neighbouring landlord, who had been involved in civil aviation. It had been on the brink of scrappage, when on a whim, he had offered it to the boys, just to mess around with.

Except he hadn't banked on this little team getting it airborne again.

Phyll watched him as he climbed into the cockpit. She felt both excited and nervous. He was a novice and it wasn't the smoothest take-off, but after a few loops, he taxied back in, with a loud cheer from the crowd.

Family, friends and neighbours quickly surrounded him. She waved from the back of the crowd and mouthed to him. 'That was brilliant!'

He grinned and nodded back, and later when all the fuss had died down, he whispered conspiratorially: 'Fancy learning yourself?'

The rest is history. Phyll took him up on his offer and their courting sat side by side with this new venture; that is, until the announcement of war accelerated a wedding date. She remembered that day so clearly, with its blue skies and white clouds. She was under no illusion about the risks of marrying an aviator. They managed a quick ceremony, a photograph and it was all over in twenty minutes. FLASH! The bulb discharged amongst the bouquet of pink carnations.

Indeed, the ink was barely dry on the marriage certificate when the newlyweds were separated, Eddie being stationed for service at RAF Fighter Command

She remembered how she felt after waving him off from the platform. A mixture of emotion and determination. Indeed, she was still wrapped in her coat when later that afternoon, she found herself pacing the farmhouse parlour floor.

Now Eddie boy. You're going to have to forgive me!

Her pen scrawled across one, two, three pages, her brow crinkled with concentration. Every so often she stopped and looked out from the window. A black bibbed sparrow was hopping amongst the daisies; a delicate ball of feathers, foraging for food. Then it was gone; soaring and swooping on its beautiful wings, startled by the whistle of a train in the distance.

Her hands were shaking when two weeks letter she opened the envelope from the Ministry.

8th August 1942

Dear Mrs Edwards,

Thank you for your application to the newly formed women's section of the Air Transport Auxiliary. Your letter is certainly of interest to us, particularly your number of flying hours and varied experience. Your references are also to our satisfaction. As a result, I will be able to offer you a position as a cadet trainee pilot in No. 6a Ferry Pool at Mayfield on a months' probation.

Before joining us, please do try and arrange your own billet. If you are unable to do this, I can book you a room at the Grape's Hotel for a few days, giving you the opportunity to look around yourself for suitable accommodation.

You will be issued, on loan, with a flying kit and your pay will start from the date upon which you join.

I trust this is to your satisfaction.

Yours Sincerely,

G. P. Marshall (Adjutant)

Phyll's telegram to Eddie was short and sweet:

Been accepted by the Air Transport Auxiliary. STOP Surprised but delighted STOP

She wasn't sure why she felt surprised. She supposed it was because it just hadn't occurred to her that she *would* be accepted. Things had moved so fast since the outbreak of war. Women flying as part of the war effort - who would have thought? It could be a chance to feel useful, to be able to contribute in the best way she knew.

***

Captain Hadley scanned the group. A new round of recruits and there wasn't much that missed her. She reminded herself of why she was doing this; for all the others that had lost their lives in this dreadful war. She leaned on her stick. Damned leg! It was a bitter blow that she could no longer get airborne. A crash had ricocheted her into ground crew. It has also bought her a badly set leg and burns to the back and neck.

Still, she would turn out the best pilots to grace the earth - if it was the last thing she did.

'When will be up in the Spits Ma'am?'

There was a murmur of excitement from the group.

V was sitting at the end of the assembled row, legs crossed, blond hair coiffed into her not so straight hat. They had been at the aerodrome for six hours; they could at least have had the drill by now. She sensed rivals all around. Here was a group of girls who could already fly like her, probably acing at other things too.

V's invitation from the Ministry had arrived out of the blue. In many ways she was still in shock. One day she had been engaged in the most delicious love affair and the next she was off, roaring towards Mayfield, engine at full throttle.

Surprises can invigorate life and V had always lived large. The war had not stopped her enjoyment of dinners, dates and dancing, not even the Blitz. In fact, V had just spent the previous few months in a haze of ecstasy, sipping martinis and rolling around under the covers of blackout. Her latest squeeze being of particular interest.

But then the letter arrived: brown, official, with HMS stamped in red across the front. They noted that she held a pilot's license and would like to know if she was interested in joining the ATA.

This was the news she'd been waiting for. There had been rumours of course; arm twisting to put women in the pilot's seat. But no one quite believed it would come true.

Marvellous!

For one moment she thought of her new beau. *What a shame*; he's *so very exciting.*

But of course, there was nothing that would come between V and her chance to fly again.

***

The captain flicked ash into a tray behind the lectern and weighed up the girl with the unsolicited question. Entitled - yep that about sums it up.

'Like Spits, do you?'

She tapped the floor and there was a moment of silence as she scanned the room.

'Indeed Ma'am.' *Damn it! It was a reasonable question.*

The captain smiled, a tight-lipped smile that seem to stiffen her jaw. V waited for an answer, but it did not come. Instead, the captain nodded towards the rest of the group.

'Good evening and welcome to Ferry Pool 6a!' She coughed and cleared her throat. 'Well first the good part - well done for getting this far. Be proud because it's some achievement. Each of you has been selected because you've already shown potential as competent fliers. That's a great start.'

She paused. This was what she needed, a new team, a new beginning. 'These pools are 100% essential. Here you'll be trained on the Class 1's from Tiger Moths to Harts, Hinds and the Avro Tutor. If you get through that little lot, you'll then advance onto Class 2's and so on. You'll be flying aircraft straight to the squadrons that need them.'

There was a renewed murmur of interest around the room.

'There will be great flights and not so great flights, you will need to understand everything and I mean everything about weather, maps and navigation. The training will be arduous; you'll be tired, shattered, pushed to your limits! BUT,' the captain paused, and took a breath, 'if you ever doubt yourself, just take a look out there.' She pointed her cane to the window and at the shadows of aircrew moving silently to and from the aerodrome.

'Day and night, they're out there, sortie after sortie. Never has the need been greater for us to pull together.'

That seemed to break the ice and there was a spontaneous burst of applause.

'I like her style,' whispered Phyll to Jane Harrison who were both seated at the edge of the row, closest to the window. 'She doesn't beat about the bush.'

'Now in terms of the practicalities,' the captain continued. 'You need to be carrying a gas mask and only a few of you seem to have one. Please make sure you are issued with one in the morning. There will be a series of exercises to represent attacks. I'll run over the rest of the procedures tomorrow, but for now,' said the captain brushing ash from her sleeve, ' back to the machine of all machines!'

She turned and pointed her cane to a picture behind her. A Spitfire in all its glory - soaring through the clouds with the sun on its wings.

The captain took a draw on her cigarette and blew the smoke to one side. 'Beautiful little thing; a plane of great sensitivity and handling, extremely comfortable, very responsive.'

The captain screwed up her eyes and read V's name off her lapel. 'Bowes-Hudson?'

V stiffened. 'Ma'am?'

'In answer to your question, none of you will be flying Spits, until you've received the bulk of your training.'

V bristled. Surely that could not be true. Why did they need to wait? 'Ma'am. With all due respect. I'm here - we are all here because we can *already* fly.'

There was a pause and some nervous mutterings. Someone dropped a teacup. *Interesting* thought the captain looking down at her notes and silently scribbling *BH* on a notepad behind the lectern. The room fell silent and a smile passed across the captain's face. She took a final drag of her cigarette and gathered some papers together, squaring off the edges with particular care.

'Congratulations!' The captain ground her cigarette into the ashtray. 'You've brought some levity to the matter. But you see it's back to basics BH, for you-for all of you. You may not be fighting in the sky, but you will be flying a much greater assortment of machines than many of our chaps out there. They'll be no shortcuts.'

V's mouth tightened.

'You'll be re-learning the rudiments, everything from sunny day flights to forced landings and how to get out of a spin........need I go on?'

You could hear a pin drop.

'As I say no shortcuts. You're up for one hell of a ride!'

Chapter Four

The cottage had a garden of old apple trees, with a front door that grated against the stone floor. Jane pushed it open. It was evening and the flagged front room was dark, low roofed and cold. She dropped her bags into the centre of the room and immediately felt comforted. The low cottage with its hipped roof of thatch, was not dissimilar to home.

V followed her in, wrinkling her nose. 'What's that dreadful smell!'

'Might be a few mice about! Come on, let's look up here!' Jane unlatched the door to the stairs.

'Who mentioned mice!' Phyll Edwards grinned and swung her cases through the door. They slid across the floor. 'I quite like the things as long as they don't get in the bread.'

'Oh Lord!' V shivered. 'It's freezing, there are probably mice and it's the size of a postage stamp.'

A short while later and Phyll was also feeling despondent. There were two rooms upstairs and she'd lost the toss for the smaller one. This meant she would have to share with the woman who was currently fussing over a trunk of fine tailored gowns.

Phyll grimaced to herself and then started to fold some woollens into a drawer.

'You've come prepared!'

'Well we may be staying in Topsy Turvey Cottage,' observed the woman who was now unfolding a shimmering green gown from the depths of her trunk, 'but that doesn't rule out possible invitations to more salubrious surroundings!' V was feeling somewhat put out. Sharing a room might be wearisome, especially when on inspection, it had an angled ceiling, which she was bound to bump her head on, plus very little room for the storage of her large collection of outfits.

'Please be a darling and pass me one of those hangers.'

Phyll laughed. 'You're welcome. I've only got two skirts, one to fold and the one I'm wearing!'

Jane could hear everything through the thin partition of her small front room and smiled at their conversation. *It's certainly going to be cosy. Good manners will be an absolute necessity!* She placed her sketch books neatly down on her dressing able and popped some brushes into a jam jar that she had found on the window ledge. Satisfied, she took a look around her small box room. Small, but perfectly adequate she thought, shutting her door quietly behind her and knocking tentatively on theirs.

'Are you decent in there?'

'Yes darling!' replied the girl with the large trunk of clothes. Jane stuck her head around the door and smiled.

'It's a bit of a squeeze isn't it!'

V reached for an extra cardigan. 'A chilly squeeze!' then added: 'Given our proximity, I think we'll be seeing a great deal of each other, decent or otherwise!'

***

A young Polish pilot by the name of Kowalska and a fresh-faced boy of no more than eighteen sat in the wooden barrack room alongside the new Ferry Pool. Kowalska had flown in Poland and the boy was straight from cadets. A few months of training and they would be up in Spits, scrambling with the rest of them.

It was seven in the morning and ATA ground instruction on mathematics, navigation, and the principles of flying were all to take place, side by side, with the pilots who continued to scramble both night and day.

'Count yourself lucky you'll be starting at that time,' the captain had pointed out to the newly formed group. 'It's a luxury.' Indeed, by the time the new recruits were dressed, breakfasted and ready for their first day, the pilots, who had risen at dawn, were already by their own aircraft, ready for action and waiting for the order to scramble.

'Pilot's notes,' said the captain swinging a spiral bound notebook. 'Sized to fit inside the knee pad of your flying suit. This is your new best friend. Each card gives concise information on speeds, power settings, plus other vital info for a whole range of different aircraft. Have a quick look and put it somewhere safe.'

'Thank you, Ma'am,' Hattie Sykes screwed up her eyes and brought the pages close to her face.

'We need to do something about that. When was your last eye test?'

'I...I don't remember Ma'am.'

'Give me strength! How did you get recruited! No matter. Go down to supplies later, they'll arrange a medics appointment. I'm sure we can sort something out.'

'There are always prescription goggles,' came the voice with the clipped vowels. 'My brother used them.'

'Yes, thanks Cadet. Let's leave that decision to the medics, shall we?' The captain reached inside a wooden crate. 'Now - compass and gyro. More essential parts of your armoury. I think you can see how few navigational devices you'll have at your disposal.'

'What about radios?' asked V turning a compass around in her hand.

'None issued I'm afraid.'

'Unless you're in a squadron.' Kowalska added.

'That's different. Of course.'

'Why is that Ma'am?' V looked around at the rest of the group. 'Seems to me that one might be in a spot of bother if anything went wrong.'

'Fighter pilots get priority,' noted the captain. 'Resources are limited. Perhaps they will come our way at some point. But, for now, you'll just have to keep your wits about you and make sure you learn the drill. This is in case of any issues either with the engine, or any potential obstacles. Assume you are on your own out there, which for the most part you will be.'

***

'All I'm saying girls, is that we *will really* need to know our stuff. Ferrying aircraft seems to involve all sorts of potential hazards: absence of radios, the danger of stalling, stopped propellers and the risk of barrage balloons.'

Brenda Johnston stared at her plate under the bright lights of the Salvation Army canteen; boiled potatoes and a slab of something unidentifiable.

'By the way, is this some sort of ham?'

'Yes lovely!' Phyll handed her plate over. 'Pass it over if you're not eating it. Waste not want not!'

V rolled her eyes. 'Roll on next month when we can eat in the Mess. Goodness knows why we have to eat here at all.'

'Now come on lovely,' Phyll admonished. 'It's not so bad. It all goes down the same way! Don't be such a snob!'

'One simply gets used to certain things.' V announced grandly. 'Perhaps they expect one or two of us to leave by the end of the month. *Perhaps* the captain thinks it will be too tough for some of us.'

'Nonsense.' Phyll laughed. 'She has everything to gain by seeing us all through this.'

'Agree,' nodded Hattie Sykes, helping herself to another slice of bread. 'It would reflect badly on her if we flop the training.'

'I still maintain,' said Brenda adamantly, 'that we will have to be utterly prepared. The captain has certainly opened my eyes to the hazards of ferrying all these aircraft about, especially, the danger of stalling and stopped propellers.'

Hattie scraped a small ration of spread onto her bread. 'Oh how I miss butter!,' she laughed, pulling a face. 'By the way stopped propellers shouldn't be a problem. Provided you have sufficient height, a dive with a fairly sharp pull-up should restart the prop and re-engage things.'

'And what about engine failure?' Jane stood up with her tray. 'Do we bail or force a landing? I'm not sure which would be the safest! Let's just pray we don't find ourselves in that situation. Pudding anyone?'

'*Sí, por favor,*' Maria Pérez picked up her spoon, adding: 'There'll be incidents, I'm sure. It's unavoidable, especially given the numbers of drop offs we'll be expected to make.'

'Well, whatever happens, I am sure we'll do it with style!' V picked up her tray and started to edge her way towards the plate stacker.

'That's the least of our worries!' Jane called after her 'There are too many ghosts for that!'

***

Autumn is the poet's season, ripened fruit, golden leaves and a month of mists.

It can also be cold in the heavens.

'Back to a freezing, open cockpit!' observed V, who had

already graduated onto closed models in her previous flying life.

It was their first day of flying and the captain was giving the briefing.

'Make sure you're wearing two pairs of socks,' she instructed, 'I won't be doling out basins of hot water for when you come back.' She tapped her cane against the side of a Tiger Moth.

'Squadron Leader Hicks will be your instructor. He'll be in the front; you'll be in the back and dual controls *will be* engaged.'

'Absurd, quite absurd!' muttered V under her breath.

Hicks was a tall man, in his late forties and with a tendency to shout caused by partial loss of hearing, the consequence of many years near loud engines.

'The advantage of an open cockpit, especially for training, is that it's easier to bail out if something goes wrong!' he bellowed.

'Hooray to that!' nodded Hattie enthusiastically.

'But more difficult if you're short like Harrison!' teased Phyll.

Jane dug her in the ribs. 'Watch it you! Actually, it's completely true! I'll need at least two cushions stacked behind me!'

'Ok, well we can get those, no problem. You can go first - let's see what you're made of?'

'Sir?'

'Step onto the wing, and get that parachute folded in. The rest of you can wait inside.'

'Good luck!' V snuggled into her flying jacket. 'I'll watch from the window.'

'Settled in Harrison?' asked Hicks looking up. 'Here grab these.' He passed her a couple of bolsters, dark green like the colour of the wings.

'Thank you, Sir.'

Hicks hauled himself into the front seat. 'Now I know you've flown solo, but I just want to see what you can do. Give it your best shot.'

Jane took a deep breath and started her pre-flight checks: harness, hydraulics, oil. Satisfied, she leaned over to the waiting mechanic and lifted her thumb.

'Contact!'

The mechanic swung the propeller and the engine roared to life.

Adjust to 800rpm, watch oil pressure. Check! She opened the throttle and the little plane, with its yellow underbelly crept forwards; rocking backwards and forwards as it rolled across the springy turf. At the end of the runway, she turned the little aircraft into the wind, and waited.

'Good. Now steady her and keep the aeroplane straight and level!' called Hicks from the front.

Final check, she thought, moving the throttle fully forwards; *oil pressure holding steady*. She started to accelerate, applying gentle forward pressure on the column control to raise the tail.

'Keep straight with the rudder Harrison. Tail up!'

As she moved forwards, she felt the rhythmic whirring as the wheels bounced off the grass and then she was up!

She was airborne!

There was an intoxicating smell of cut grass, oil from the exhaust stacks and a swirl of slipstream about her.

'Good work,' called Hicks. 'Now twice round and try a glide.'

'Sir.'

She looped around the aerodrome and then powered back to idle moving into the glide. The little canvas plane soared weightlessly through the air. She could see for miles; the railway line, forest, river and the aerodrome, with its criss-cross patterns of tracks and scattered buildings. Dispersal was everywhere, but autumn had stripped the leaves off the trees and both aircraft and structures were quite visible now: hangers, workshops, fuel stores, bomb stores. For a moment she had goosebumps:

We're sitting ducks down there. No amount of camouflage

is going to disguise the fact that this in an aerodrome.

The instructor reached for his notebook and she steadied herself.

'Ok Harrison. Take her down.'

With the throttle closing, the plane started to descend, and when the speed dropped, she lowered the wheels and taxied back in.

'Not bad. A few things to work on, but otherwise, pretty faultless.' Hicks jumped down and headed off to the dispersal room. 'I'll be back in ten minutes,' he shouted behind him.

Jane felt a surge of relief. She hauled herself out of the cockpit and slid off the wing to the ground.

'I need heat!' she said, smiling and clapping her hands together as she came through the door of the Nissan Hut.

'Well done Harrison!' Phyll Edwards slid her a chair across the room. 'I'd say that was textbook! Any tips?'

'Just get it straight before take-off. Oh... and check how many pairs of socks you're wearing. It's freezing up there!'

Verona Bowes-Hudson stood stiffly by the window: *late autumn; damp boots, steamed up goggles*. She felt inside her jacket pocket and for the fragment of her brother's tattered scarf between her fingers.

This was not an easy time of year.

Hicks pushed open the door. 'Mary Miller?'

'Sir!'

'You're next, follow me.'

Mary strapped on her helmet; her auburn hair now encased in brown leather and sheepskin trim.

'Here,' said Jane. 'Take an extra pair of gloves. One pair doesn't cut the mustard.'

'Thanks.' Mary took the gloves and slipped them on.

'And good luck,' said Jane rubbing her hands by the stove.

Chapter Five

'You'll need to focus with this one,' remarked V to the others, one early November morning as she climbed down from the Harvard's cockpit. 'It requires a delicate touch!'

'Happy to take your advice!' nodded Jane as V swept past, unbuckling her helmet. In truth she was a little in awe. The girl was very smart. She had good technical knowledge and was a natural behind the joystick. She had scored top marks for most of the training flights, despite the fact it was her first experience on nearly all of them.

Now Jane was out solo too, picking up the Magister and settling behind the de Havilland Gipsy Moth engine.

She methodically went through her pre-flight checks, remembering the advice of the instructor:

'It can be fairly unforgiving on take-off. Just hold her steady.'

She started the engine and the aircraft shook into life. Carefully she eased on the controls and it started to move, picking up speed and bouncing on the tarmac as she pulled the stick for take-off.

As it rocked a little she muttered to herself: *Come on now. Keep her level!*

It was a relief once she was airborne, Take-offs often caused her stomach to flip, but she had to be patient - they were all progressing at different rates. V and Hattie Sykes were stomping ahead; with Johnston and Edwards not far behind, but herself and Maria? Well, they had started with the least flying hours, so they were always going to be playing catch up. Lastly, there was poor Mary Miller. She was struggling, had made several nervous mistakes and was now under review.

Still she had graduated from the Tiger Moth and now she was flying this beautiful little plane. It was more modern than the Tiger Moth; it had brakes, flaps and a tailwheel for a start.

She pushed the little plane on through the clouds. It bounced along on its spruce frame, the wind whipping her face, the sun catching the top of her cheeks and the bridge of her nose.

For a while she flew in such conditions, until she hit a patch of rough weather and suddenly the visibility was poor. It was always a surprise to her that the weather could turn in this way. For a while she found herself weaving in and out of heavy cloud formations, relying on the iron bars beneath her and the navigation aid strapped to her knee.

It had been a long flight back from the manufacturing unit. She felt in her pocket for a small square of chocolate and let it melt on her tongue. *Bother! I wish there was more!* Suddenly, she realised how cold she was. *These rudder bars are freezing!* She couldn't even feel her toes.

At last, there was a break in the clouds and they started to tear up, drifting off like shreds of candyfloss. Familiar landmarks came into view: the water works, the village school, the church spire. She began the deceleration. At 60 knots, she set the flaps down, the airspeed tapered off and she dropped the nose, banking towards the landing strip.

Something didn't look right. It seemed far more active than usual. Lorries and trucks were racing across the grass and people were running in all directions.

Then it hit her, the deafening wail of the siren.

The Harvard bounced on the ground and rolled to a stop. She could hear the Tannoy but it sounded distorted, drowned out by the sound of the chaos around.

A sergeant was waving at her.

'Get out Ma'am. Fast as you can!'

She quickly unbuckled her harness, but before she had even finished, Phyll had emerged, scrambling onto the wing.

'Hurry! *HURRY WILL YOU!*

'What's going on? Yes, yes I'm coming.''

'No time to explain. Just get yourself out!' She was already grabbing her arm. 'Word is …'

She didn't finish because at that moment the voice of the controller came over the airwaves and this time there was no mistaking what was being said:

'*Large bombing formation approaching Mayfield. All personnel not engaged in active duty take immediate cover!*'

'GET A MOVE ON HARISSON!'

'Coming, coming!' Jane was half dragged off the plane's wing by her friend.

'Come on *RUN*. We need to get to the shelter!'

They ran as fast as they could, the roar of engines behind them. Along one of the three point landing strips, four Spitfires had turned about, roaring past them for take-off. They ran, half clutching into each other, a gleam of metal

in the sky heading ominously towards them. A dozen dark shapes, shining in the daylight, and moving at speed.

'Oh God Phyll, they're coming!'

'Get to the Blast Pen!' shouted a Warden indicating vigorously in their direction.

There was a sickening sound, as the defending Spitfires were catapulted apart. The leader flipped over on his back and ploughed along the perimeter road with a crash of tearing fabric, whilst the others were scattered across the fields - one immediately bursting into flames.

The cadets shot down into the shelter and were met by several voices in the dark.

'Get your head between your knees, hands at the back of the head!'

'Hold tight everybody!'

For a while, the noise was horrific; sounds of whistling and whining and the shelter heaving at each explosion.

It seemed to last for ages; dust falling on their heads; thick and choking.

Then as quickly as it had started, it stopped and there was a long anxious pause in the darkness.

'All clear, I think!' came a nervous voice.

'Open the door Sprigsy!'

The warden made his way back up the steps.

'Gas masks on if you have them,' he shouted back.

The door was pushed open and light flooded in - streams of it, illuminating the fifteen of so bodies crammed into the dark, dank space below.

'Out you come!' The warden shouted. 'There's work to be done - but be careful!'

Phyll and Jane held onto each other as they stepped back out into the open. Devastation was everywhere, gaping holes and mounds of earth, trucks on their sides and aircraft in pieces, shouts and cries from the injured.

'We must help.' Jane started to walk quickly towards a young man lying on the grass. He stared at her like a rabbit caught in headlights. There were wounds to his stomach and legs.

Jane knelt beside him. He let out an agonising moan.

'It's ok. You'll be ok. The ambulance is on its way. Stay still now, there that's it.' She looked at the blood spilling from his leg and seeping through his jacket. 'We need to bind him up.'

'Check your top pocket' Phyll kneeled next to her, opening his top button. 'Should be a field bandage in your flying suit.'

'Yes, yes of course. I forgot,' said Jane finding the waterproof packet in her breast pocket. 'We must stop this bleeding.'

'Hush, hush you'll be alright.' Jane soothed, grasping the packet and tearing it open. She pulled out a large pad, wrapped into the middle of a strip of thin fabric.

'Wrap that leg wound well Janey.'

'We need something for his stomach. That wound looks pretty nasty.'

'Coming straight up. Hold on boyo.'

Jane worked quickly. She made a tourniquet for his leg and bandaged him as best as she could. He looked so young, just a boy.

He stared at her. He was still whimpering, but the sound was diminishing and his eyes were starting to shut.

'What's your name? she asked urgently. He must stay awake.

He couldn't hear. There was pain in his ears and only muffled echoes of sound.

'Hey, don't close your eyes now. Try and stay with me.'

She looked about, no sign of any stretcher bearers yet. Fires were burning and water hoses were being unravelled.

When she looked down again he had closed his eyes.

Phyll returned, flushed in the face. She threw down a sandbag, a sheet and a blanket

'Couldn't find much, the huts are firewood. How's he doing?'

'Not so good. Any sign of an ambulance?' Jane began to rip the sheet into shreds, while Phyll began to empty some of the sand out from its bag, keeping the rest to fill the sheet.

'Not that I can see.'

'Ok, we'll just have to get on with it. Put the little bag down gently Phyll. Nice and easy now.'

Carefully they placed the make do sandbag over his stomach. For a while, the blood rushed out and around it. Then it began to slow down.

'Put the blanket over him Phyll. We need to keep him warm.'

They covered him up to his neck and waited. Jane holding his hand.

Someone was reading the roll call and orders were coming through quickly. The stretcher bearers had arrived and were ferrying the injured to the waiting ambulance.

'You've done well,' remarked one of the medics, as they lifted the young man into the back and under the painted canvas.

'Here take this.' Jane handed them the blanket. 'Will he be ok?'

'It's difficult to say Ma'am. Watch your back now!' He indicated to let her know that more stretchers were coming through.

'Where are you taking them?' she called, as she made way for the next casualty.

'It'll be St Ambrose.'

Jane nodded and turning to Phyll said: 'Let's find out who he is.'

It had started to rain. Phyll turned to look back at the aerodrome. It was decimated, with smoke, craters and destruction everywhere. 'Let's hope he's lucky Janey because something good has got to come out of this day .'

***

Phyll poured the tea. 'I've put sugar in. It may help with the shock.'

'I think we'll need it,' Jane sipped. It was hot, sweet and comforting. 'What a day. It was horrific and that poor young boy. He barely looked out of school.'

Phyll rested her feet on the grate. The fire was still a little insipid. 'Pass me the bellows lovely. We need to get these flames going or they'll disappear.'

It was late and they were cold and exhausted. They had spent most of the day in convoys, moving rubble from various points around the aerodrome. They had watched unexploded bombs being tapered off and yellow flags being erected, lining the newly tarmacked runway, now full of pits and craters.

Despite their exhaustion they had managed to organise a wash of some sort, in an old tin bath that they had dragged in front of the fire. It was a rigmarole that took a couple of hours.

Boil water, wash, refill, repeat.

'We're the lucky ones.' Jane took another sip of the hot, sweet tea. They were shattered and shaken, but they had both escaped remarkably unscathed. - V too, who had been lying on her bed with a headache. She had come into land a couple of hours later and had to make several attempts to avoid craters.

Phyll nodded. 'Five dead and twelve wounded at the last count. I wonder how our boyo's doing.'

'He was in a bad way, poor thing. He didn't look much more than a youngster.'

'Well we can find out a bit more in the morning; there may be some news then. We didn't even catch his name.'

'Aircraftsman Tommy Mitchell,' said V, as she came down the stairs trailing a blanket off the bed.

'He's the new boy in Hanger 2.'

'Well, that will make it easier when we try to find out how he's doing. Jane passed her a cup of tea. 'Here, we saved you a cup, but it may be a little cold now. How are you feeling?'

'Horrendous headache darling.' She flopped down onto the rug near the fire. Her face catching the glowing heat. 'Still at least training's been grounded for the week.'

'Really?'

'Yep. I caught the captain on my way back. She was a bit of a mess, cuts to her hands, legs. She was still bossing everybody about though.'

'Well I hope you said something nice V,' commentated Jane in all seriousness. 'That sounds terrible.'

'I did actually,' V smiled, her lips still smudged with the remnants of the cherry red lipstick which she applied as a daily ritual whether she was flying or not. 'I said bad luck,' and then she added aloofly and with an even broader grin, 'and what's the itinerary for tomorrow.'

'You didn't! Jane tried not to laugh. 'Honestly, V. Couldn't you have said something a bit nicer?'

'Such as?'

'Oh, I don't know.... I'm sorry to see you've been hurt. Hope, you feel better soon? You know that sort of thing. You're going to get slung out if you don't watch your mouth!'

'Nonsense darling! They need every one of us!'

'Except poor Mary.' Jane drowned the last dredges of her tea. 'Word is she's been sent home.'

'Now that *is* a shame. She was a darling dancer and huge fun!' V rubbed her toes; a quarter of cross countries completed, and she'd been half frozen on most of them.

'It is a pity. She was a good pilot too, just made a few mistakes that's all.'

'Can't afford those though can we.'

'V's right Janey.' Phyll agreed. 'Mistakes can be dangerous - to ourselves and others.'

'I suppose.'

V smiled. Her cheeks becoming pink by the firelight.

'Well, listen girls. I for one, am really looking forward to flying the Proctor.'

Phyll nodded. 'We need something to look forward to. It's got a closed cockpit hasn't it?'

'That's why I'm looking forward to it! It will be a hell of a lot warmer to fly!'

Chapter Six

A week off training and it was just what they all needed. There was still work to be done, but it was a different sort of work.

It was a cold, late November morning and Jane was making her way across to the guard room The rumble of tractors continued to move, lay, relay, patches of the aerodrome.

'Any chance of a connection?' asked Jane, poking her head around the door.

'Certainly, Ma'am? 'answered the duty sergeant. 'Location?'

'Reception at St Ambrose. We'd like to know how Tommy Mitchell's doing.'

'Right you are. He'd only been with us a week, poor lad. Give me a minute and I'll connect you.'

There was some brief conversation over the exchange and then he handed the receiver to Jane.

'Good Morning. Sister Mary Angela speaking. I hear you're inquiring about Aircraftsman Mitchell?'

'Yes, that's right Sister. He came in injured from Mayfield.'

'Indeed, he did and I am told you are one of the young ladies, who helped him .'

'Oh goodness, yes well we tried our best Sister. How is he?'

'He is recovering well and making good progress. It's early days, but he is as comfortable as he can be.'

'That's marvellous news.' Jane put her thumbs up as Phyll's head appeared around the door. 'May we come and see him?'

'Not yet I'm afraid; there's still a risk of infection. Give it a couple of weeks. He should be over the worst of it by then.'

'Of course. We'll do that and thank you.'

'Good news all round then,' observed the sergeant, rescuing the receiver from her hands.

'It couldn't be better!'

'He's not out of the woods yet Janey,' pointed out Phyll, 'he was badly injured, remember.'

'Yes, but he's young, he's strong. Hopefully, he'll pull through.'

'Well I'll second that!' Phyll stepped back outside adding: 'Because we all need a bit of cheering up.'

Jane thanked the sergeant and followed her outside.

'Are you ok Phyll? You haven't looked yourself lately.'

She linked her arm though her friends, as Phyll shook her head.

'Come on let's get some fresh air.'

They found a bench that had been hastily erected by the

newly repaired canteen and sat down. Phyll dug around inside her pockets, pulling out a crumpled piece of paper.

'It's from Eddie.'

'Is everything ok?'

'You can read it if you like,' said Phyll sniffing and reaching for a handkerchief and a crumpled piece of paper.

The page was damp and the ink smudged, but the message was clear enough:

Thank you for your letter my love. To be honest things have been desperate here. Empty chairs in the billets-you know the score. James, Paddy, Peter-all gone.

Having survived the Battle of the Skies thus far, I'm now to be transferred.

Of course I am unable to say where to, but a good guess might assume that any letters may take a very long time to reach you.

All you need to know is that I love and miss you.

Jane folded it up and handed it back.

'I'm sorry Phyll. Of course, you're bound to worry.'

'I do and all the time now.'

'Look I know it's not much comfort, but you've always said that Eddie can get out of any scrape.'

'I may have been exaggerating, 'replied Phyll miserably.

'Now I don't believe that for one moment!' Jane gave her a reassuring squeeze. 'He's a brilliant pilot. He'll be alright.'

'I hope so, because I really need my Eddie.'

'I know. Come on, let me help you take your mind off it. How about giving our rebuilt, remodelled canteen a try? My treat.'

Phyll blew her nose. She felt better. Sharing things often had that effect, despite the fact that they were often encouraged to keep things to themselves.

'Ok lovely, you're on. I'll try anything to stop fretting.'

***

'Anyone home?' Jane sunk wearily into the battered armchair with its faded pink print.

'Just me!' Phyll appeared through the back door, shivering and a little irritable. 'Lavatories should *not* be outside! It's freezing!'

'You're right,' Jane unlaced her boots and held them near the fire. 'It's pretty grim in that little shed and everything is so wet at the moment too. It looks like the brook has burst its bank, maybe in the last half hour or so. It was spilling onto the lane. Wow watch the steam come off these boots!'

'Everything's wet through lovely: kit, clothes, towels, linen. We need a dose of Maria's Spanish sun to dry things out! Oh the joys of an open cockpit!'

'Agreed! Flying is hungry work too! I'm famished. Are there any of those jam buns left?'

'Do you mean my eggless wonders? Yes I think so. I'll fetch some and make us some cocoa too. And get your socks off Janey, or you'll catch a chill.'

Phyll stoked the stove in the kitchen and poured some milk in a pan to boil. She warmed her hands on the range as she watched it heat up.

'Only a month or so in and it's killing me!' Phyll stirred the drinks and handed one to Jane. 'Wouldn't it be nice to have just one day off.; just one little day.'

'Doubt that will happen.' Jane hugged her knees and rubbed her toes. 'Not with the continued assault on the ports and an insatiable demand for new planes to be collected. No, I think we just have to accept that it's going to be like this for some time.'

V walked in fifteen minutes later, muttering, cranky and wet.

'It's pouring out there and the water in the lower lane was up to my knees!'

'I'll move the sandbags. Better to be safe than sorry.' Phyll pulled on her wellingtons. 'It was up to the front step last time it rained like this. There's cocoa in the pan V. Grab a cup and come and sit down. You look done in.'

'I've had better days darling. All I can say is that it's going to be fun with the captain tomorrow!'

'Oh V! What have you been up to now?' Jane passed her a towel.

'Went for a loop as one shouldn't,' smiled V squeezing the water from her hair. 'Propeller stopped and I went into a spin! Fortunately, I remembered how to recover and managed to restart the engine.'

Jane shook her head. 'How on earth are you going to get that past the captain!'

'Agree! She won't be too pleased. You were lucky; it could have ended so differently.' Phyll tutted and shook her head.

'But, it's such fun if one can pull it off!' V took a sip of the cocoa.! I was rather hoping no one would notice.'

Phyll erupted with laughter. 'Rubbish! If it had worked, you would have wanted everyone to notice!'

***

'Captain's ready for you now. Ma'am.'

'Thank you, corporal.' V walked in, stood to attention and saluted.

'At ease BH.'

The captain looked through her notes. ***Idiot,*** she thought. *Two weeks back in the saddle and the girl had come unstuck **AGAIN**! Granted she's an excellent pilot, but she really does think highly of herself and this last caper was something else.*

'I think it's fair to say BH, that you've outdone yourself this time.'

'Ma'am.' V nodded, looking straight ahead. How was she going to get away with it? She'd already had a ticking off about her illicit loop the loop, now she was really in trouble.

If she had only not misjudged that damned field.

V's live for today attitude was both a blessing and a curse and when one day a party invitation had come her way, well - it had been too good to miss.

It was an invitation from retired Brigadier Naper and his wife who lived in the old Rectory at the far end of the village. They wanted to help the station. Morale was low, with the aerodrome having taken a hammering and the invitations had been sent out on the back of this. They were keen to use the excuse of a party to invite the tired and shattered aircrews for respite. Of course, there was rationing, but Mrs Naper had whisked up some treats with the help of neighbours and the invitation had been too good to miss.

V had flown miles that day but she was determined to make it back. They had promised champagne and not a drop had passed her lips for months. How could she resist?

Blow! She thought as she attempted to land her plane in a near the Rectory. *I just need a field with a good long run!*

Of course, it didn't turn out like that. V overshot the long field and bumped her Magister into a small patch of rough land. The machine hit the chilled earth, spinning at a right angle and coming to rest - wing to gate.

'Damn it!'

'***BOWES-HUDSON****!'* The captain was incandescent.

'Did you not consider for one moment, how you were going to get that aircraft **OUT** of the field?'

'To be frank Ma'am. I thought I might come up with some ideas during the evening.'

'You're an absolute idiot! A sensible person would have drawn a line on a map and then followed the compass back to base. But YOU! You decide to throw out the rule book and take a little detour! There's absolutely no room for horseplay. Pilots can get into any amount of danger, crossfire, misjudged landings, entanglements - from telegraph wires to barrage balloons.'

'Misjudged landing Ma'am. I....'

'Stop there!' The captain bristled and held up her hand. 'Hold it right there and let me finish the story for you.'

V's luck had run out. It had seemed such fun at the time, but judging by the look on the captain's face she was in a whole heap of trouble now.

***

'Anyone want anything?' called Brenda Johnston. It was Hattie's birthday, and they were calling the rounds at the local hostelry: the Fox and Crown.

'Gin and tonic darling!' shouted V across the long bar.

'Martini cocktail, please Bren,' called Maria who was deep in conversation with a WAAF, whose arm was in a sling.

'So, come on V, what happened?' asked Jane.

'I've been given another chance darling.'

'Lucky blighter,' laughed Hattie.

'Yes, but with conditions attached!'

'Such as? Phyll was in raptures. If anything was going to cheer her up this story was.

'Firstly, I had to agree to talk to the farmer. I had to persuade him to make a space in his hedge in order to facilitate a long enough run to get the Magister airborne again.'

'And secondly? asked Phyll with tears rolling down her face.

'Well secondly I had to agree never to use service equipment for personal use again.'

'Oh Lord V, that's a given!' Brenda brought the drinks to the table. 'And did you get the Magister out?'

'Done and dusted. I managed to dragoon a couple of mechanics and they helped me. They used a tractor and undertook a bit of levelling work too.'

'You're a damned marvel V.' Brenda raised her glass. 'How did you get the farmer to agree to that?'

'Mmm …well I may have bent the truth slightly. I told him that I'd crashed into the field, which in a way I had.'

'That's a lie and you know it,' laughed Maria coming over and joining them.

'Desperate measures darling, and I think my contract was on the line.'

Phyll shook her head. 'I'd say you've had a lucky escape. I think the captain would happily see the back of you if not for the fact you're a damned good flyer. Look what happened to poor Mary!'

'You're right darling. Best behaviour from now on!'

'Well, I've got a bit of news,' smiled Jane, the sherry warming her through. 'I'm picking up a mystery visitor tomorrow!'

V's ears pricked up. 'How delicious! Tell us more.'

'Well, I don't know much more, except that he's coming by train. His name is *Dr Richard Reynolds.*'

'And what are you to do with *the Reynolds*?'

Jane laughed. 'Not a clue! All I know is I'm to take him to lodgings at the Rectory, then show him around the area - give him a bit of a tour, including the base. That sort of thing.'

'Well, we will want to know everything.' Maria savoured the last few drops of her cocktail. 'Every little bit!'

***

The first Friday in December and the last of the falling leaves were tumbling off the trees. Rooks circled like smudges of ink in a grey sky and it was one of those days when it never seemed to brighten up.

Jane was waiting for the 11.10 from Paddington. The platform was deserted except for a few sparrows pecking at crumbs by the station master's house. She had positioned herself at the end of the platform, hoping that it would not be too difficult to spot her passenger, for she had little information about the man she had been asked to meet. All she knew was that he was to be billeted with the Brigadier and that he was an academic of some sort.

Jane smiled. The girls would expect the low down tonight.

She saw the train long before she could hear it. It was clearly visible amongst the forest in the distance; whirls of smoke were billowing above the tree tops. Then with the distant sound of pounding pistons, hissing steam, and whistles, the train clunked into the station and came to a screeching halt.

She needn't have bothered with the sign that she'd made. There were only three people who stepped off the train. A young boy with his mother and a man, older than Jane had expected; around thirty, maybe mid-thirties. It was difficult to tell. He was tall and pale with a head of unruly brown hair and clear grey eyes that seemed to look right through her.

He carried a packet of notebooks and a small leather case.

'Dr Reynolds ...Dr Richard Reynolds?'

She met him halfway down the platform. 'Pleased to meet you Sir. I've been asked to pick you up and take you to your billet.'

The man looked puzzled and placed his bag down, drawing his coat about him.

'*Er* - Thank you' he replied hesitantly, casting his eyes immediately down and muttering almost inaudibly, 'I wasn't expecting any sort of reception party.'

Richard Reynolds was not in a good place. He had recently secured a research post at Cambridge but had been ill and was still feeling the effects of the low mood that had descended upon him.

For a while he lingered, with those thoughts in his head.

Jane waited, a little confused. She didn't like bad manners in anyone. *Rank really can bring out the worst in people* she thought, feeling a little irritated.

'May I help you with your bags?' she continued, a little shorter in the voice. 'I can drive you straight to your billet. I believe the Brigadier and his wife have arranged refreshments.'

The visitor, sensing tiredness and hunger, nudged himself into the present and looked up. He realised that he had been a little abrupt. He met her eyes and began to falter. 'Er …yes…well… kind of you to arrange. 'Thank you…er….?' His mouth stretched into a stiff smile, but it didn't quite reach his eyes.

'Cadet Harrison, Sir,' she replied briskly. 'The car's just this way.'

He picked up his bags and began to follow her back to the car. Jane retrieved the key from the top of the front tyre, opened the back door and then made her way around to the driver's seat.

She started the engine, not sure whether to speak or not, but soon decided against it. He did not seem someone open to small talk. The car moved off slowly, crunching over the gravel and up onto the lane. Soon the fields swept by in a patchwork of russets, golds and greens.

Not a word passed between them and neither did he observe the direction in which they were going. But, he did notice soft brown curl escaping from her cap and resting against the blue of her collar.

Chapter Seven

I've the perfect tonic for a miserable December!' V burst through the door, the raindrops still in her hair. 'Tickets for ENSA! These should cheer us up!'

'Brilliant! Do you mean, 'every night something awful'?'

'Now come on Phyll, that's hardly fair! Who are we to judge if we've never even seen them?' pointed out Jane. 'It's a great idea.'

'Thanks. I think so. By all accounts, the Entertainments National Service Association is a fine outfit!'

'Depends on who you talk to lovely.'

'Oh, come on, don't be such a square!'

'Ok…Ok. You've twisted my arm. When's the show?'

'Tomorrow evening. Lots of our boys will be there. So, it' will be worth a pop!'

Jane and Phil looked at each other and rolled their eyes laughing.

'Ok V,' said Phyll rolling her eyes. 'We'll keep you company!'

***

The message reached the other girls, who unlike Phyll, V

and Jane were debunked to an annex on the ground floor at the back of the Officers Mess. It was adequate, but cold and a little damp. Brenda and Hattie seemed to be able to put up with it, but Maria was not impressed.

Maria's parents had come to England from Madrid, when she was fourteen and she missed 'that glorious weather'. When it was especially cold, she would sleep in her underclothes with her pyjamas on top, cursing the chilly nights. This was particularly so when it was time for 'ablutions' (as the other girls called it). She would run along the damp and narrow duck boards, clutching her towel and sponge bag and cursing the cold grey mornings.

Brenda, Maria and Mary Miller were lounging in a small room off from the Mess dining room when Hattie Sykes popped her head around the door, flourishing a handful of small blue scraps of paper.

'V's got a bunch of free tickets to see a show tonight. Anyone want to come?'

Maria nodded. Suddenly she felt a little brighter.

'*Si*, I *love* such things!'

'Here you go, one for you!'

Brenda lifted her head from her book. 'Throw one this way Hattie. It might be worth a shot. What's it about?'

'I'm not sure it's about anything in particular. It looks like a variety performance.'

'It says ENSA' Maria inspected the small, printed ticket. 'Looks like it's in the entrainments building.'

Hattie laughed. 'Well, let's just hope the piano has been

tuned. It sounded awful the last time I heard it being played!'

'It's something to do,' observed Brenda, returning to her book. 'Something to take our minds off how tough these last few weeks have been.'

***

The 'Ents' building was simply a large space inside a marquee at the back of a hanger. It had been decked out in full Christmas regalia; with holly and paper chains made from old newspapers and a large tree that had been cut down from around the back of the airfield and which was now festooned with dried fruit and knitted decorations sent from friends and relatives to the base.

There was quite a crowd, with the audience being directed to their seats; long rows of benches with a stage at the front and some makeshift curtains.

'Hola!' Maria called seeing her friends.

Phyll and Jane waved back 'Hola lovely! Where's the rest of our lot?'

'On their way. Hattie is fetching snacks and Brenda had a phone call to make. I've saved you a place!'

'Excellent,, thanks Maria! Now where's V?' Jane looked around. 'Ah, there she is! Deep in conversation!'

Maria laughed. 'With a very nice gentleman!' They could see their friend quite clearly, her hair teased into victory rolls piled high upon her head and her shoulders shaking with laughter at something she found clearly amusing.

'I think both she and we will have fun tonight!' Maria was excited. The atmosphere and anticipation felt familiar. It was the same feeling she had experienced as a small child, when her mother would take her to watch the plays in the wonderful *Teatro Español*. She recalled the gasps of excitement as the curtains swished back to reveal the beautiful sets of the Spanish classical theatre. She had never forgotten that enchantment.

The music started with a drumroll, the lights dimmed and the curtains swept back to reveal a small four-piece band with a violinist, cellist, and a pianist with a poorly strung piano.

'Ladies and Gentlemen!' A young man with a heavily powdered face stepped onto the stage. 'Please put your hands together for our resident band…. The Dixie Marsh Bells!' There was a loud cheer and much whistling, and the band started, swinging straight into a tune and a medley of songs.

It was Maria who remembered most of it afterwards: 'a tenor and soprano singing a duet, a magician with a box of tricks, a dancer with a performance of Swan Lake's Odile…..'

'A comedy sketch performed by three men with an assortment of hats!' interrupted Brenda, in raptures.

'A stand-up comedian…whose jokes were so bad that he was nearly booed off the stage!' Hattie shook her head, laughing.

A final curtain call and a medley of all the hits from the show and then it was time for the bows and goodbyes and a standing ovation from the delighted audience.

The subdued lighting lifted and the crowd began to make its way out and melt away. Phyll stood up and stretched her legs.

'That was brilliant; just what the doctor ordered!'

'It was a tonic alright! Pretty good actually. How about continuing the hilarity back at the Mess Bar?' Hattie was feeling thirsty.

'Count me in!' Jane looked around. 'Let's see if V wants to come.'

Phyll spotted her a few rows back. She was edging herself back out, along the benches still deep in conversation with the young man from before and who they now noticed was still dressed in his flying suit.

She spotted them and waved.

'I may be a while longer!' she called over. 'I've a date for this evening!'

Phyll shook her head, laughing. 'Who's the lucky fellow then?'

'Fordy.' He nodded and smiled, as she hooked her arm through his. 'A navigator too! Very nice, don't you think!'

'Just a bit!' laughed Jane.

'Has he got a friend?' winked Hattie. 'For Cadet Harrison here?'

He laughed and called back. 'Definitely! Want me to arrange something?'

'No I do not!' laughed Jane, going red in the face. 'I'm far too busy for romance at the moment. Things to do, planes to catch!'

The friends gathered together outside. The sky was overcast and they were happy about that. Clear skies were always far more worrying.

'Come on, let's go back to the mess bar. It will be a hundred times warmer than out here.' Hattie stamped her feet against the ground. 'We can look forward to V's stories later!'

Phyll laughed, shaking her head. 'I don't think so! I think we will have to wait until tomorrow for those!'

***

'How about a spin to Lincoln?' The Navigator had caught up with V as she came into land. They'd only had a few dates and he was already smitten.

'I have a rest day tomorrow. Are you free?' He grinned broadly.

'A spin? That sounds intriguing.'

'On my motorbike.'

'I'll look forward to that.'

'Fuel rations, damned nuisance. I would have taken you in the car otherwise.

She looked at him as she took off her helmet and shook out her hair. He had come straight off the bombers and still had the maps in his hand.

'Motorcycles are more fun. I'm on rota tomorrow, but free the day after.'

She glanced at him side on. He looked tired, drawn.

'How's it going up there?'

'Don't ask.' His expression clouded over. 'We lost a crew over the Channel last night.'

'That's ghastly.'

'Yep. We could both do with a break from this endless nightmare.'

'I'm not arguing with that.'

'I'll see if I can do a bit of arm twisting for Wednesday then?'

'Marvellous!'

His smile returned. 'Pick you up about nine, provided the arm-twisting works!'

She stopped, and looked at him, sheltering her eyes from the bright winter sun . 'I guarantee it will work.'

Chapter Eight

It was dark by the time Jane got back to the cottage. It had been another full day; three drops offs and two pickups; a Miles Master and a Hawker Hart, trainers for the constant supply of RAF recruits. It felt like she had been ferried about in the Avro taxi all day long

She changed, had a wash, and rinsed her hair. Flying made you filthy.

V and Phyll were not back, so she made a pot of tea, sat by the window and turned on the radio, *Vera Lynn* was presenting *Sincerely Yours*. Jane turned it up and stoked the fire. Thank goodness it had stayed smouldering. It was one of the few comforts of the cottage; courtesy of the farmer who owned it and the provision of an almost constant supply of firewood.

The heat started to make her feel drowsy. She pulled a blanket around her and stared into the fire. Outside she could hear an owl hooting, getting ready for a night of flight. Her mind drifted to Richard Reynolds. It was doing a lot of that lately. How many times had they been out and about? Trips to the Hangers, trips to dispersal points, trips to the Mess, tea with the Brigadier. They had talked and compared notes; weather, maps, navigation and had wholeheartedly agreed on their desperate wish for the war to end.

'How long are you here for?' She asked him one day, quite out of the blue. It was nearly the end of December.

The berries clung to the mistletoe and the snow was starting to fall. It drifted in banks along the runways and made heavy work of take-offs and landings.

'I'm not sure …. until I manage to solve a few technical problems, but you know how it goes. No one knows what's really happening from one day to the next.'

She nodded. It was late afternoon and they had taken a stroll through the lanes.

'Let's jump in here for a bit Jane. It's really coming down now!'

They sheltered in the porch of a church, watching the snow drift and blow across the carved stone arches.

'On second thoughts let's go in.'

It was dark and quiet inside, with a sweeping arcade of pillars and round arches. There was an altar in the chancel and a cluster of candles burned in the corner, the yellow beeswax dripping over the sides.

They lit candles and sat quietly, thinking of all those who had lost their lives in this ghastly, dreadful war. There was a smell of incense and seasoned wood and the sound of the wind in the trees outside.

'It's peaceful in here,' he whispered and then hesitated, 'thank you Jane.'

'For what?' They sat shoulder to shoulder looking up at the stained-glass window.

'For being such good company, for being here, for looking at this beautiful window with me. For just well you know...'

'It's no trouble, honestly. Glad to have been of help.'

Over the past few weeks Richard Reynolds had begun to open up, or at least he would start to. He would tell her just a little, then always stop - just short of what she felt was *really* bothering him.

Because there *was something*, she just couldn't put her finger on it.

'That window is similar to the one at Magdalen.'

'Magdalen?'

'It's a college at Cambridge.'

'You must be clever to be there.'

'Not really.' He coughed and shifted in his seat.

'What's the nature of your research?'

'Engineering,' he paused, not wanting to elaborate further, then added, 'I managed to win a late scholarship there.'

'Why late? What did you do before that?'

'So many questions!'

'I'm curious,' she said, digging him in the ribs.

He smiled. 'Ok, I was in the RAF.'

'I knew it!' she exclaimed out loud and then lowering her voice added: 'I knew there was something!' she then whispered, in somewhat euphoric tones at having stumbled on part of the mystery: 'Only someone who had flown before could understand the technicalities of flying the way you do.'

His smile disappeared a little.

'What made you stop?'

He did not answer and she knew he would go no further.

'Let's head back now,' he said, standing up and wrapping the scarf around his neck. The shadows of snowfall had stopped falling behind the coloured glass.

She touched his arm and stayed sitting. 'Richard,' she said softly.'

He stiffened a little and sat back down.

'A problem shared is a problem halved?'

'Indeed,' he said, turning to look at her. 'It's just....' he hesitated; he still couldn't talk about it, not yet anyway. 'It's nothing of any importance.' He shook his head and changed the subject. 'Anyway, what about you? What's your story? After all you've achieved something wonderful. So many pilots - so few women. You'll make history!'

'Goodness, I'm not sure about that, but it has been a long journey and we're doing our bit. Come on, I agree. let's go now, before we get snowed in completely!''

They left the church, shutting the heavy oak door behind them and headed down the snow filled lanes. The drifts were backing up against the hedges and for once the world seemed still and quiet.

He still wanted to know how she had come to fly. What had brought her to Mayfield?

They carried on talking, heads down, collars up against the wind.

'Where did you learn to fly? How did you get into it?' He asked as he took her hand to cross a stile.

She told him some of it. How she had worked in her aunt's shop in Rye to pay for lessons and how thrilled she was when selected for training with the ATA. She told him of V and Phyll and the 'ATTA' girls, how she missed her mother more than anything and how she worried about her father.

'And where is your father?' he asked gently.

'Away.' She replied bluntly. For a while there was silence, but when she spoke again there was a break in her voice, as she pushed on, head down, through the snow.

'He was a pilot, had flown in the '20's - Sopwith Camels moving onto Hurricanes. He was nearing the end of his flying career.'

'You said *was* a pilot?' He held back, but she kept walking, tears stinging her eyes.

'Jane?' he caught up with her. 'What happened?'

She stopped and looked at him. Suddenly, it seemed such an intimate moment to share with someone she barely knew.

'I'm sorry. I shouldn't have asked.' He could see she was upset.

'It's ok-truly,' she said, unconvincingly, turning and walking onwards. She didn't want him to see her like this. For a while she just focussed on the crunch of the snow beneath her feet. It soothed her and when she spoke again, she sounded more composed.

'He was catapulted into war over France. He has been declared missing,' she paused. 'Presumed dead.'

'I'm really sorry to hear that,' he said quietly, catching up with her. 'Must be awful for you.'

'For Mother too, she's desperate about him.'

He caught her arm. 'Come on, let's go back.'

She nodded and felt the warmth of his hand through her coat.

'You're freezing! Here have my coat.' He pulled it off and wrapped it around her.

'Thank you,' she said looking at him. He was so close that she could hear him breathing. He smiled and blew on her hands, rubbing them with his.

'Cold fingers,' he said wrapping his hands around hers. The warmth of them permeated her own and accompanied an unmistakable sensation; that of her heart beating faster. She could tell by his face, that he had felt it too.

'Come on,' he said trying to dismiss it. 'Let's get back before we freeze out here.' He started to head off but she stopped him.

'Richard?'

He looked at her. Her brow was furrowed and her eyes filled with questions.

'Yes,' he answered, dreading that she might ask him about that moment. But she didn't and for some unknown reason, he breathed a sigh of relief.

'Do you think there's any chance that he maybe….'

'Alive?' he said, finishing the sentence for her.

'Yes,' she said quietly. 'You see I really believe that there is.'

He didn't want to tell her what he really thought.

'Perhaps - yes. Of course, there's every chance.'

She nodded, not sure why she had sought his opinion. She now felt a little exposed, nevertheless she took his outstretched hand, as they approached the last stile.

'Do you know anything about it all?' He asked gently as she climbed over.

'Nothing whatsoever. But…. I *will* find him or at the very least find out what's happened to him.'

Richard nodded. He didn't want to say that the odds were stacked against it. Instead, he grabbed the wooden post and hauled himself over the stile after her.

***

Jane's father, Squadron Leader Gerald Harrison was battle weary. August 1939 was to be an important month and year. He had plans and had been looking forward to the end of his flying career and to a less transient time. There had been talk of a possible air ministry post that would have allowed him a 9-5 existence and more time at home, where he and his wife were looking to rent some land and run a small livery stable.

But then the shadow of another war approached.

Duty called and Harrison quickly shelved any winding down plans and when Blitzkrieg began, he was plunged into the thick of it, and posted to France where he was deployed mainly along the Belgium-French border.

New orders came through and his Squadron was sent to Reims where he was caught up in an ugly scramble. They fought with all the skill they could muster and at first things looked like things were turning their way.

But then his luck ran out.

It happened within minutes followed by those odd few seconds when pain doesn't register. One moment he had been weaving at speed through the sky, the next his aircraft had come to a juddering halt, hit by a stream of bullets.

For the briefest second, time seemed to stand still. His thoughts drifted as the shot tried to take him, and for a while, he felt he was watching fireworks shooting in the sky all around him.

'Come in Number One, Come in Number One!'

The voice drifted through his head, like wind whistling past his ears.

Then another judder of bullets and he was brought to his senses.

I must get out!

His mind started to trace the steps he needed to take. Tracer bullets streamed past him and for a brief second the Hurricane was on its nose and he was looking straight down thousands of feet below. There was no way of pulling out of the vertical and smoke was now pouring from the nose of the aircraft.

He knew it was now or never

'Come in Number....'

The radio crackled to a stop. He grappled with the harness, blood spilling over his hands. The pain in his chest threatening to consume him.

He could see the tree tops. With one last pump of adrenaline he pushed the canopy open, falling freely into the night air.

Was it the forest that saved him or the distance he landed from the plane? He spun around, half conscious, the parachute billowing above him and watched as his plane plummeted below, crashing to the ground, a great ball of fire shooting into the dusk.

His fall was broken by the outstretched branches of a tree and for a while he hung there, the pain in his shoulder making him throw up. He felt his head pounding and his eyes shutting. He had to stay awake. He heard voices; soldiers calling to each other some distance away. They had seen the plane go down. With a last burst of strength, he managed to unbuckle his chute and drop to the ground. A pain shot up into his stomach and he felt himself retching onto the damp earth. The voices came closer and then within moments they were upon him as he drifted into unconsciousness.

When Harrison awoke, he could not tell where he was. He certainly was not in bed at home. Indeed, he wasn't in bed at all. He could smell hay. An early morning breeze was blowing through the cracks in some wooden slats above him. The light was hazy, but he could make out a blue sky through the holes in a red tin roof. He heard the clank of a pail and somebody climbing a ladder. A hatch opened and the face of a young woman appeared, brown eyes staring out from under a shock of short curly hair.

'Bonjour Monsieur! Un peu de lait?'

He tried to lift his head but found he couldn't move.

'Bonjour. Where am I*? Où suis-je?'* He scrambled to remember the snatches of French he had been asked to learn.

She smiled and climbed into the hay loft. She wore a pale faded print dress and grubby plimsolls. In her hands she carried a pitcher.

'You are in my barn and quite safe. You were found by my compatriots.'

She placed a glass next to him and crouched down, pulling his blankets back a little.

'You were found in a field. Your plane crashed. You were taken to a house and how you say? Patched up? You stayed there for three days. Then they brought you here.'

'Three days?'

'*Oui*, you have been asleep Monsieur.'

He felt his chest. It was heavily bandaged.

'Come on you must eat and drink.' She poured some milk from the jug and put her arm around his back, raising him just enough for him to take a sip.

'There, we must make you strong again!'

'*Merci*,' he said lying back down; the room was starting to spin.

'What is your name?' he asked weakly.

'I am Claudette.' She wrapped the blanket around his chin again. 'And yours?'

'Gerald... Gerald Harrison.'

'Well, Monsieur Harrison. It is no longer your name.' She smiled. 'Bonjour, Monsieur ...whatever your new name will be!'

Chapter Nine

January and it was unusually wet. The first week of 1943 had bought snow, but this had now melted, dissolved under the driving sheets of rain.

Two figures were weaving through the lanes on a motorcycle. The day had dawned a little brighter and for once there was a break in the clouds, the fragile sun catching the gleam of metal as it streaked past fields and hedges.

A young woman was out cycling, on her way to the nearest farm. Winter jobs included clearing some small branches and trees of which she and some others were set to do that morning. Behind her, she heard the throaty sound of an engine approach. She dismounted and leaned into the hedge with her bicycle.

The motorcycle slowed down and both the driver and the passenger waved in thanks as they passed by, taking care not to splash her. She noted that the passenger wore a bright red scarf and that it was billowing exotically in the slipstream behind her.

Once passed, the driver opened his throttle and they were away again. 'Flying' as V liked to describe it, 'but in a different way.' She felt exhilarated. It was just what she needed. The hedges were a blur, the fields changed like patchwork and the villages became larger as they approached the outskirts of Lincoln.

Soon they were slowing down and weaving in and out of the narrow streets, heading down towards the river. Bomb damage was evident everywhere, particularly to the houses around the edge of the city, residences that were in close proximity to an airfield, not far away.

It was a stark reminder of the intensity of the night raids.

'We'll pull in here!' the Navigator called back, slowing down and coming to a stop in a spot by the river.

'Hope that blew a few cobwebs away!' he said unbuckling his helmet and making a point of *not* mentioning the shattered buildings they had just seen.

She leant forward and hugged him.

'That was perfectly marvellous!'

'Good. I'm glad,' he said leaning back and kissing her. 'Now come on, let's explore and make the most of it.'

He had parked his motorcycle by the entrance to the river footpath. Or at least they guessed it was. Every street sign had been blacked out.

They linked arms and made off down towards the river, soon finding themselves quite by accident, at the entrance to the Arboretum, with its tranquil ponds, bridges, and gardens.

They instantly felt the peace of the place. Winter still shrouded the lawns and there was a greyness to the pruned back roses and wisteria vines, but there was a beautiful stillness about it all. Even the roses without blooms looked magnificent. The dark green leaves sparkled with the rain that had been unseasonably heavy these last few weeks.

The navigator held out his hand and she took it to follow the paths that twisted and turned, eventually taking them out onto the streets and up to the cathedral with its gothic arches and stained-glass windows.

They explored the beautiful grounds outside, wondering through the cathedral quarter and noting the construction of a large water tank, which the fire service had built should airstrikes hit the cathedral.

Inside they marvelled at the sweeping arches and vaulted ceiling, joining a small group to admire the beauty of the rose window in the south transept, radiant with colour in the near darkness of the nave.

They moved on, listening to the hushed voices around them and lifting their heads to get a sense of the height and space of the place. For a while, they stopped and prayed; kneeling amongst others who had also sought refuge in the comfort of the cathedral's hallowed walls.

Later, when the skies clouded over, they found their way to the Picture House, where they bought sugarless Bath buns and laughed their way through some slapstick comedy, until their sides ached.

'Brrr! It's freezing!' exclaimed V, as they stepped back outside, adjusting their eyes to the daylight again.

He took off his jacket and wrapped it around her shoulders, pulling her close to him.

'Better?'

'Much,' she said kissing him. 'Thank you James. I've enjoyed myself so much. It's felt a million miles away from the madness of our lives at the moment.'

'You're right.' He grinned. 'Thanks for taking up my offer.'

'A pleasure Sir,' she said kissing him again.

'How about taking a final walk back along the river? If we go now we might catch supper back at the Mess.'

She agreed and so they set off again, retracing their steps through the cobbled streets, until eventually they found themselves back on the towpath.

They stood to let a small group of boys whizz by on their bicycles, laughing at their enthusiasm and plans to make mischief. Then they set off again, along the river, hand in hand, swinging their arms between them.

'Can we sit for a bit?' The young navigator asked after a while. He had a question. This was his one chance, having avoided asking it earlier for not wanting to spoil things. 'I need to ask you something.'

V guessed at what it might be and she braced herself.

They found a bench, and sat, bodies touching, looking across the water to a pair of swans, orange billed and snowy white, gliding gracefully towards them.

The navigator had saved a little of his breaded bun from earlier. He tore a piece off and threw it into the water.

'Wish I had something better for them, proper seed for a start.'

'It is pretty impossible to get your hands on that at the moment.'

He smiled as they swam towards them side by side, eager to grab the scraps of food.

'They're love birds V!'

She laughed. 'So they are!'

'Listen V,' he continued, looking straight ahead and not wanting to make too big a thing of it, 'there have been rumours.'

'How delicious,' she pronounced, trying to lighten the conversation.

'Rumours, that you're on the move.'

'Yes, that's right. News really does travel fast!'

'Always,' he said, dropping his head a little.

'I'm sorry,' she said, squeezing his arm, then adding playfully. 'Will you miss me?'

'You bet I will. You are a rare find Verona Bowes Hudson.'

She kissed him on the cheek. 'Well that's good then.'

He felt a little despondent. She knew how much he had fallen.

'Look darling, we have only just found out. It's the conversion course to Class 2's. We don't even know when or even where we are going *and* we should be back once it's done.'

'It's marvellous of course,' he said, finally turning to look at her, and taking both her hands in his. 'It's great news for all of you. It's just that...'

'I know.' She squeezed his hand. 'Chin up darling.'

'Damn it V, I'm going to miss you - I mean ***really*** miss you. You see I've fallen a little in love with you.'

V threw her head back and laughed. 'A *little* in love! One simply falls head over heels or not at all!'

'Then it's the former.'

'James!' she said half smiling, half admonishing. 'There's a war on out there. There's no point in getting over our heads. We simply don't know what's happening from one day to the next.' Then she added a little more tenderly, 'let's just enjoy each precious moment together and have a little fun. Yes?'

He squeezed her hand and nodded. 'Of course, we always have that.'

'There you go then.'

He sighed: 'You will keep in touch won't you ?'

'I promise darling. Now stop being perfectly silly and let's get home before blackout.'

He smiled feeling brighter and jumped up, holding out his hands to pull her up.

As they veered off the footpath and up towards the road, she suddenly had a thought. 'We'll be having a leaving do. You will come won't you.'

'If I must,' he smiled as he unlocked the engine. 'But only,' he added as he handed her a helmet, 'if I get the first dance and maybe even the last one!'

'You'll get both of them Flight Lieutenant,' she agreed climbing on behind him, 'and every other dance in between, but *only* if you take me home the long way round.'

Chapter Ten

'Class 1's complete! Broadlands here we come!' Phyll tossed her cap into the Mess lounge and raised her arms in jubilation.

Training was progressing, having all swept through these last few crazy months. The Mayfield Six now knew where ***and*** when they were going.

Additionally, in honour of this achievement they were to be measured for some new uniforms; with a trip to London for fitting. Something that the commanding officer had arranged.

Phyll was jubilant. She pulled Jane up from her chair and the two started to dance across the floor, with Jane laughing so much, she felt her sides aching.

'Look how far we've come Janey

'Never doubted it Phyllis Edwards!' They spun around like two giddy school children.

'Pipe down will you!' grumbled Brenda looking up from a game of chess.

'Checkmate Bren!' triumphed Hattie, moving her queen to bishop.

'Blow! It's so difficult to concentrate when there's such a din going on!'

Hattie smiled and leaned back in her chair. 'A poor chess player always blames others for their lack of concentration.'

Brenda scowled, 'Okay! You've won. But I'll get you next time!'

'Fighting talk, Brenda Johnston,' retorted Hattie laughing as she packed away the little wooden pieces.

V smiled to herself as she bent over to the gramophone where the sublime tones of *Anne Shelton* were playing on the old wind-up. She was more than a little amused by their rivalry.

She picked up the needle and the music came to an abrupt stop.

'Stand by for announcement!' pointed out Brenda, standing up and stretching.

'Indeed!' said V with a playful look on her face. 'I vote that we make both a day *and night* of it in London. We should make the most of it.'

'Really V,' laughed Hattie. 'That's hardly an important announcement!'

'Ah, but it is,' Maria was on V's side. She needed cheering up. *England could be so grey*: 'Transport leaves at 2pm tomorrow afternoon. A night in London would be perfect!'

'Good that's settled then.' V was already on her way out, with every intention to pick out the perfect gown, 'and look *FABULOUS* everyone!'

The ride to London ended up taking four hours; far longer than it would have done in peace time. Constant detours due to problems *en route*, extended the journey, but this did not dampen their spirits and it was an animated group of cadets who jumped out of the truck the following day. They were out of their routine and although this felt a little strange, it was nonetheless, exhilarating to be doing something different and getting a new set of clothes, even if it only uniform.

They found their way to the prescribed tailors on Ludgate Hill; a bespoke outfitter, with a rich history and now supporting the war effort.

V was the first to comment on entering the establishment and observing the rolls of serge material now pushed to the front of the counter.

'Oh bring back the days when one could order something ravishing for everyday wear!'

The tailor, used to such high flown ways in this establishment, remained impassive. Expecting this group and already prepared, he spread a measure of material onto the counter top, to which he added for buttons and a brass buckle.

'Single breasted with lapels, ' he said inscrutably, moving the material this way and that way to show them how it might all look together 'four buttons and a fabric belt with a brass buckle. Your uniforms will be very smart.'

Jane felt the dark blue material between her fingers.

'Can't wait.'

V's attention was now elsewhere. 'Is there any chance of a little extra?' she inquired, looking behind him.

'Extra?' asked the tailor looking up.' He saw the pale eyes of the tall girl eyeing up a small roll of his best silk.

'Yes, a little flash of red fabric? In the lining for example?'

'It could be done,' he looked down and continued cutting. 'For a price.'

'Oh, come on girls, let's leave V to her wheeling and dealing!' said Phyll laughing and opening the door onto the street 'No one but you could think of adding a red lining to the inside of your uniform.'

'At my expense darling. One has to do things in style!'

***

The Commander wanted to acknowledge the importance of the first groups of women to be signed up to and fly for the ATA. He had therefore, arranged some rather special accommodation for the Class 1 graduates.

The Grand London Hotel would host Brenda, Maria and Hattie. The establishment was happy to provide accommodation and a special night's stay for such 'brave and dutiful members' of the Air Transport Auxiliary.

Meanwhile, V, Phyll and Jane were to have a different arrangement. They were to be lodged with the Buchanan's, a Whitehall boffin and his wife who lived in a very elegant Nash terrace near Embankment.

The press seemed particularly interested in them to and later on that afternoon, when ensconced in a hotel lobby with pots of tea, they were approached for a story by a young man from a local newspaper.

The girls insisted categorically that they could not give interviews, but still the young man persisted and the questions came thick and fast:

Is it correct that you are supplied with a small suitcase with toothpaste and pyjamas for overnights stays?

Is it true you have to be over 5 ft 5 inches tall and between 20-28 years of age?

Is it true you have to use clothing coupons to buy your own uniforms?

'***STOP!***' Hattie had tears in her eyes from laughing so much. 'These are really the most ridiculous questions and of course we can't share a thing with you. Ask out captain, she may be able to give you more detail.'

The young man, good humouredly accepted defeat. 'Ok I give in! You must admit though, it would have made the ***most*** brilliant read!'

***

The bus ride to Embankment was a slow and unsettling one. The ride, taking them to the north part of the Thames, revealed the after effects of the Blitz. Months of bombing had brought an odd juxtaposition, people hurrying about carrying out their normal late afternoon activities, amongst piles of rubble and crater filled streets.

Life trying to carry on regardless.

Phyll stared out of the grimy windows. 'What a mess! How much longer can it continue.'

'Any respite can only mean that they've turned their attention elsewhere.' Jane felt a shiver down her spine. 'Next stop please!'

V rang the bell. 'Yes, almost certainly to that poor lot in the Atlantic.'

They found the house quite easily. V knew this area of London well. It was a smart residence, tall and quite narrow, with an elegant gate and steps up to a large front door, painted a deep maroon colour.

Inside Dr Buchanan had heard the approach of voices. He was a shy man, not normally comfortable with visitors, but these he had made an exception for and both he and his wife were keen to help. He chewed nervously on his pipe and pulled the door wide open.

'Welcome!'

He faltered a little, hesitating over his next choice of words.

'Indeed, you are!' exclaimed his wife excitedly, emerging from behind. 'Don't just leave them standing there Geoffrey! Invite them in for goodness sake!'

'Thank you!' said the group in unison, grateful for the warmth inside. 'We really appreciate this,' added Jane as their host took their hats.

'Not at all. We have been really looking forward to it, especially as we've heard so much about you from the commander. Do come and sit down. Make yourself at home!'

They were waved into an elegant room full of fine furniture, with several small tables scattered about.

'I've prepared a little supper. I thought you might appreciate something before your trip out tonight.'

'We most definitely would!' Phyll nodded approvingly.

'That's what I like to hear, guests with a hearty appetite! Geoffrey, can you organise drinks whilst I see how far things have got in the kitchen.'

The Buchanan's were kind and generous hosts, doing their best with the little food they had and as Mrs Buchanan poured the tea, she told them how much they wanted to help, how they appreciated the challenges of flying; the risks involved.

'It can be treacherous,' said Jane passing around the plates, 'and we had the most hellish winter. BUT it is also a great adventure!'

'Absolutely' V agreed.' We never know where our chits will take us and that adds to the intrigue. We just have to keep our wits about us that's all, especially when visibility's poor!'

'Oh yes of course. Indeed, only the other day some poor chap got tangled in one of those barrage balloons around Southampton; brought the whole plane down. The pilot was…' Mrs Buchanan stopped mid-sentence, her voice starting to break.

'Oh, I *am* sorry. I didn't think I would get quite so upset again.'

'It's ok dear', said the Doctor gently, leaning over to catch her hand, 'and apologies.' He took a deep breath. 'You see we lost our son.' There was a pause. 'He went down in the Channel.'

'Oh we *are* sorry to hear that.' Jane spoke for all of them. 'So sorry.'

The doctor looked at his wife and then at the group.

'He managed a mayday, and he did bail out, but by the time they reached him, he was under.'

'How awful for you.' Phyll said quietly.

'It was truly awful. He was the light of our lives.' Mrs Buchanan sniffed into her handkerchief.

'But we carry on as we did before and help in any way we can' added her husband.

'That's true dear,' Mrs Buchanan sniffed, 'and that is why we are more than happy to have you here.' She took a deep breath and dried her eyes. 'Now I really must apologise. What must you be thinking! I'm spoiling the tea.'

They ate quietly and the food was soon finished off.

'Thank you! That was wonderful.' V dabbed her mouth with a napkin.

'Quite delicious!' agreed Jane.

'You're very welcome. Now please do be careful tonight. The air raids here have been simply dreadful.''

'Now Moira. You're scaring our guests.'

'No, it's fine, we'll be very careful.' Jane took a final sip of her tea. 'To be honest we may not be out for long at all.'

'Nonsense Janey! Don't be such a square! We will be out as long as we can get away with it!'

Phyll laughed. 'You're SUCH a bad influence V!'

'You can count on it! With only one night in the bag, it's time to show our American friends just how fabulous we really are!'

'Well, I've only got eyes for Eddie. I'll take a couple of dances and an early night!'

Jane laughed. 'I'm not sure that's going to stop V is it.'

'I don't know what you mean darling!' V sighed, feigning surprise. 'I'm a complete innocent, but I'm going to do my hardest to have the best time!'

Mrs Buchanan smiled. She hadn't felt like doing so for some time. *What a breath of fresh air it is to have young people in the house again,* she thought.

Upstairs Jane smoothed down her dress. It would have to do. She turned this way and that to get a better view in the mirror. It was the only thing she had remotely suitable, a simple back sheath dress with a ruched waist - suitable for parties, funerals and Christmas. She twisted to the side; she'd lost weight. Flying was physically hard, there was barely time to sit down and eat a decent meal.

She began to apply a little lipstick. A dab of powder and she gave herself a nod of approval. What would Richard

Reynolds think of her now? She blushed. Why did she keep thinking of him?

There's no point fooling yourself Harrison, she muttered. *In the process of following orders, you have unwittingly allowed your heart to run away with you!*

***

The girls stood together on the footway of Waterloo Bridge and watched as the lights of London went out. One by one, as each switch was pulled, until only a sprinkling of lights were left, almost like fireflies, until they too flickered out.

Carefully, they made their way along the kerb, following the painted lines until they reached the door of the Claremont Theatre where they were met by a concierge and the rest of the group who were waiting for them in the entrance.

'Look at you BH!' Hattie twirled her round. 'You're a marvel. I'd be freezing in that!'

V smiled. Her scarlet dress, floating in the draft of the lobby. 'I'm hot bodied darling!

Hattie loosened her shrug. 'We'll soon all be that! I've heard these dance halls are packed!'

The concierge pushed himself back out through the revolving doors to inspect the front of the building. 'Good - no lights showing.' He came back inside. 'It's a clear night, never good news. Come this way please. We need to get you down to the basement.'

He led them over the carpeted foyer and around to a side area where there was a flight of steps.

'Hold onto the banisters. It's dark!'

The girls made their way down. They could hear music and it grew louder, until at last they burst through the doors, to a cacophony of sound.

'Good old Herbie!' Brenda winked as she was immediately asked to dance by a beaming American serviceman.

'Who's Herbie?' Maria shouted, looking for a table.

'He's the Home Secretary. He's said it's fine for dances to carry on.' Hattie looked about. 'Come on let's dance!'

The room was heaving, groups were chatting and drinking around tables, which had been pushed to the side. In the middle was a large wooden dance floor where couples swirled around, dancing to the music; some of the tunes lively and swinging, others seductive and slow.

One by one they were swept up. Jane was scooped up into the arms of an American soldier who had loosened his wool necktie. 'It's as hot as back home!' Brenda was in full swing with the serviceman and somewhere in the crowd, were Hattie, Maria and Phyll who had danced off together. Only V was not dancing, instead she was surrounded by a bevy of young men in their best pink and greens.

'Verona Bowes Hudson. I believe I have the honour of your first dance this evening?'

A familiar grin greeted her as she swung round.

'Fordy, you're here!'

'Came as soon as I could old girl. We had a scramble and they were down a man.'

'Hey buddy. You've cut it fine. There'd have been a score of takers if you hadn't turned up!' said one of the soldiers, as they began to melt away.

'Sorry V.'

She smiled and hugged him. 'It's fine. You're here aren't you.' Then she whispered softly in his ear.

'I'm glad you came.'

'Me too,' he said kissing her gently and leading her to the dance floor.

Chapter Eleven

It was past one by the time Jane and Phyll fell out of the revolving doors, full of cocktails and fizz. V wasn't with them. They had caught glimpses of her during the evening, martini in hand swirling to the music; her blond Victory Rolls bobbing above the crowds.

But then she was gone.

The two friends weighed up the situation 'She should be ok,' decided Phyll, 'she's with Fordy. They can catch the first train back if they miss the early morning pick up.'

'*If* they miss it!' Jane laughed, pulling a shawl around her shoulders. 'Let's hope she's warmer than we are now, because it's ***freezing***!'

'Probably not helped by very clear skies. Look at the stars! Let's hope we don't have to make a trip to the air raid shelter.'

'I was thinking the same.' Jane linked her arm through her friends 'Let's walk quickly. It's so cold! By the way, she continued, 'did you manage to stop thinking about Eddie, even just for a little while?

'Mmm - nearly, but not completely,' Phyll hitched up her hem to stop it trailing on the pavement. 'Anyway, how about you? Did you manage to avoid thinking of the illusive Dr Reynolds?

'Who said I was!'

'You can't pull the wool over my eyes lovely! You turn to jelly every time someone mentions his name!'

'Well maybe I do have the teeniest, tiniest little crush on him!'

'A damned great whopping one if you ask me. Now come on, bleary head, let's see if we can hail a cab or bus. We've got a long trek back and my feet are killing me!'

The plan was to hail a cab, but unfortunately, hailing anything down during blackout proved an impossible task. Despite their low speeds, drivers seemed reluctant to stop. Walking seemed the only option, so they carried on, briskly, crossing roads carefully, though on more than one occasion, there was a squeal of brakes as they or some other pedestrian tied to cross a road and was nearly caught by a moving vehicle. The journey back proved extremely trying under cover of darkness.

They were just about to cross another wide road when Jane stopped and pulled Phyll back.

'Dd you hear that?' she sked tensely .

Phyll strained to listen. 'Yes, I think so.'

'Anti-aircraft guns?

'Possibly. Whatever it is, it sounds a long way off.'

'Let's hope so because….' Jane didn't finish because at that moment came a different sound and one much closer; a spine tingling wail, low and deafening.

'**AIR RAID**!' shouted a man on a bike as he cycled quickly past them. 'Get yourselves down to the shelters!'

Jane grabbed her friend's arm. 'I think that means the underground.'

'Lord, where is the nearest one?'

'Just follow the crowds!' shouted a man coming up behind them. 'Up this road and take the first right.'

Shadows of people started to move quickly and quietly in that direction.

'MOVE YOUR BONY CARCASS!' shouted a voice behind them. A woman clutching the hand of a small child pushed past them.

Footsteps quickened around them. The girls could hear furniture being moved and occasionally a door would open, and someone would scuttle outside clutching a few belongings.

They began to hurry, following others heading down towards Holborn.

Searchlights were flashing across the sky above.

'Give us a bit more warning will you!' shouted a man shaking his fist at the sky.

They walked briskly, following the crowd. A door slammed and a woman came out of a thin terraced house carrying a baby in her arms. 'Just when you thought things had settled!' she shouted as a clutch of sleepy-eyed children trailed after her.

Finally, they reached the entrance to the station and started to make their way down the dimly lit steps. Suddenly, from behind there was almighty roar as a nearby anti-aircraft battery fired a salvo of bullets.

The crowd started to push as apprehension turned to panic.

'Hold on, don't let go or we'll get separated!'

Phyll could hardly hear her voice above the roar and explosion outside.

***

It was a clear moonlit night and the shadows of trees flanked the avenue.

V and James Ford were strolling along, arm in arm.

How wonderful to have caught up with each other again.

'Stay for a nightcap? My brother has lent me the keys to his flat. I can run you back to Embankment later.'

'A midnight ride on your motorbike. How delicious!'

'Exactly.'

'Well, my feet do ache. I think I've completely danced them off!'

'A drink will cure that!'

They reached the door of an elegant building and took the lift to the third floor.

The flat was modern, decorated in the latest fashions, plush fabrics, curved lines and lavish accessories. Large windows led to a balcony which in normal times would have provided the perfect vista of night time London.

'The view used to be fabulous from those windows,' he said, investigating the cocktail cabinet.

'Now we have blackout and heaps of rubble .'

'Yes, but tonight we have a French 75 and I make the best ones!' he grinned, holding up a bottle triumphantly. 'I have gin, champagne, sugar. Ah! But, no lemon juice I'm afraid.'

'Soixante Quinze **without lemon** please! Perfect.'

He poured her a long drink and passed her the glass.

'Cheers darling,' he said as they clinked their glasses, and sat down together on the settee.

Softly he pressed his hand to her cheek.

'You know when all this madness is over we could...'

'Ssh' She touched his lips with her finger. 'Let's not jinx anything.'

He smiled. 'I'll change the subject!'

'Please do!'

He passed her a cigarette from a silver box. 'Ok, change of topic! Any regrets about swapping your pile in the country for a cold billet and jam sandwiches?'

V laughed. 'Not in the least!' She took a sip of the cocktail. 'This is delicious by the way. No, I can safely say it's been an eye opener!. The girls too, they're huge fun and all quite brilliant.'

'Well, here's to whatever adventures they might bring!' He knocked his glass against hers.

'I'll drink to that!' V took a sip of her cocktail. Suddenly she felt lightheaded. Was it the excitement of the evening or was it the knowledge that the excitement could end any moment? She kicked off her shoes and took herself over to the balcony windows.

'The sky is so clear tonight. Trouble may be approaching. If only I could take a peek.'

'No V. Come back here. No chinks of light remember.' He blew out a curl of smoke. 'Besides, we agreed to have a night off from this crazy war.'

She turned and looked at him, taking a long sip from her glass.

'But, that's simply impossible.'

'Practice!' he smiled.

'Well I would,' she paused, tracing her finger around the rim of the glass. 'If it were not for this ridiculous feeling of frustration.' She sighed. 'I'm fed up Fordy.'

'Hey?' He met her across the floor and encircled his arms around her. 'What's wrong? That doesn't sound like V!'

'I know and I am probably just a little worse for wear, but...' Her voice trailed off a little and when she spoke again, she sounded drawn and tired. 'You see darling. Every day, I see you - see you all, running across the grass and clambering into your cockpits. Some of you barely out of school. Sometimes, just sometimes, I wish I were doing the same - you know, doing my bit. I'm a competent flier and there isn't an aircraft I will not be able to fly by the end of my training!'

He hugged her close. 'You are more than competent. You're a damned ace!'

V smiled. 'Thank you, for that delightful vote of confidence, but is it enough Fordy? Is it enough?'

'What do you mean? Of course it is. The work you're doing is incredibly important. The Ferry Pools are keeping the pilots as safe as they can be.'

'I'm proud of that, of course. I suppose I just need to get on with this next round of training. Perhaps I'll feel more in the thick of it then.'

'Ferrying more aircraft fresh from the factory straight to where they're needed? It's vital work V. Right into the heart of the action.'

'But that's just it. I'd like to be *in on* the action.'

'I understand,' he wrapped his arms more tightly around her. 'But, whatever we do it's *Onwards and Upwards* remember?'

'That's RAF's motto!' V pulled him close. 'You've forgotten ours: Aetheris Avidi *Eager for the Air*.'

He smiled and touched her face. 'There you go see.'

They kissed and she whispered: 'You're a tonic Flight Lieutenant.

'Listen,' he said positioning her resolutely back from him. 'I need to run you back, remember?'

'That can wait.,' she said, looking into his warm brown eyes. 'Let's have another nightcap!

***

The underground was hot and crowded. There were hundreds crowded together Some with bedding, some with flasks of tea, radios and cards.

Phyll and Jane edged their way along the platform. The air was stuffy, and sleepers of all ages lay with their arms flung out, leaving a path only a yard wide along the platform's edge. Here and there were those who stayed awake, two women with a thermos flask of tea, a young man trying to read by the light of an electric torch.

'I need to sit down I don't feel too well!' Phyll's head was spinning. She stopped and leaned against the station wall.

'Come on, let's stop here,' Jane took her hand. 'We can roll our shawls - make a bit of a pillow.'

They found a space against one of the back walls and tried to make the best of it. Phyll leaned forwards resting her head on her elbows. She closed her eyes and tried not to think of Eddie who was probably in the channel somewhere, trying to fight off the impending onslaught.

She imagined him being chased on his tail, flames shooting from his aircraft and not being able to see anything but the arc of the propeller.

Or was he somewhere else? Somewhere far away?

'Eddie?'

'Are you ok sweetheart?' Jane caught her arm.

Phyll rubbed her face. 'Sorry, I was nodding off. Yes, I'm ok.' She had to pull herself together. The last thing Eddie would want is her worrying about him. She took a deep long breath.

'Our boys will see the rest of the blighters off.'

'That's the spirit Phyll.'

It was a restless night with the girls drifting in and out of sleep. The sounds of the bombs dropping seemed to go on for ages. One came very close and the noise could be heard echoing all the way down the lift shaft.

Sometime during the night Maria stumbled upon them, Hattie in tow.

'Phyll wake up. Look whose here!' Jane shook her awake.

'You look ghastly Phyll,' Hattie budged up next to her. 'You've been partying too hard!'

Phyll smiled wryly. 'I'm not feeling brilliant, but I'm very glad to see you two. Thank goodness you're safe.'

Maria's face was strained with worry. 'It's terrible out there. The sky's alight with fires burning everywhere. We lost Brenda in the scramble outside the dance hall. Have you seen her?'

Phyll shook herself to her senses. 'No lovely, the last time we saw her was inside. She was dancing with an American boy.'

'Damn it!' Hattie tried to make herself comfortable on the floor. 'It's going to be a long night; anything could have happened to her and we won't be able to start looking for her until the morning. Let's just hope she has got out of it and has found somewhere safe to shelter.'

'You're right, it's frustrating, especially as there's nothing we can do to help at this moment.' Phyll shuffled over to make more space. 'Here, have a rest. You both look done in. We'll search for Brenda first thing.'

But, it was impossible to really sleep and when they did it was full of fitful and vivid dreams. Jane tossed and turned the most. She saw her father falling from the sky over France and then her mother, who appeared to be poking the embers in the hut at the end of the garden. Miss Collins from next door was there too, *knitting squares to make into blankets for the troops and Merchant Navy.* Tears fell in her sleep.

'Hail Mary full of grace. Please keep them all safe.'

***

The all clear finally came and after a restless night, they stepped out, blinking into the shattered daylight. The constant reverberation from the explosions had made it impossible to switch off and everyone was exhausted.

The crowds that had squeezed onto the platforms, now began to melt away, disappearing into the smoke filled streets.

Smoke was everywhere, hanging like fog in the air. Carefully, they picked their way over the rubble, strewn with fallen telephone lines and twisted iron. Buildings had been reduced to piles of bricks, and water and gas pipes were fractured. Fire crews battled to extinguish flames; their uniforms soaked through.

They moved through the streets in silence, feeling sick and holding hands. They passed a church, crumbled like a pack of cards, piles of masonry from the spire heaped up in the nave. History obliterated, families torn apart and the noise of rescue, retrieval, and grief all around.

They stopped several times to help, the result being that it took them some hours to wind their way back to Embankment.

***

Dr Buchanan had been out looking for them for the best part of three hours. At some point he decided that it might be prudent to return and make some phone calls, but when he did, he was met by his wife who had discovered V slumped on the steps outside their front door.

She was covered in cuts and clearly in shock. They put their arms around her and helped her up. She looked exhausted; her face streaked with grime. The dust still appeared to be thick in her throat and she was having difficulty putting weight on one ankle.

She swayed and held onto the railings, clutching in her hand, a torn and ragged square of silk.

'Come on let's get you cleaned up dear,' said Mrs Buchanan gently putting her arm around her shoulder. 'There take it slowly now; only a few steps.'

Suddenly, from behind them, they heard a familiar voice.

'Oh, thank goodness!'

It was Jane's voice, with the other girls behind her.

V turned to look. , They were hazy in outline, but it was them alright.

'Thank God!' she cried hoarsely, trying to compose herself, feeling such relief that they too had survived.

'Poor V. It looks as though you were caught in the thick of it.' Jane hugged her.

'Come on everybody. Let's get inside. Time for catch up later.' Mrs Buchanan ushered them up the steps.

'But where's Brenda?' said V exhaustedly, looking around.

'We don't know,' said Hattie miserably. 'We lost her in the chaos. Maybe she went back to hotel. We just hope that…'

'Don't worry, I'm already onto it.' Dr Buchanan pushed open the large front door. 'I'll make a few calls.'

They gathered in the large, warm drawing room, with the fire dancing in the grate. V felt completely out of it. The room seemed to be lurching and spinning around. She closed her eyes and the night flashed before her yet again; nightcap, siren, waves of bombers and James shouting to get under the table.

She couldn't remember the explosion or how long she had been unconscious. She came to, in degrees, slipping in and out of a strange dream. She was trying to stretch her legs, but the rubble, she was partly under, was wet and heavy. The sensation of weight on her body continued for some time, until at some point, she regained consciousness and realised that this was no dream at all.

In her waking state, she became aware of a sharp pain in ankle and for a while she was afraid to move, barely aware of space or time. Then she felt drops of rain on her face, just a few and then more until a light shower fell from the invisible clouds and brought her round completely.

'James? James?' She uttered his name, but she could barely muster a whisper and with that the feeling of being alone came upon her. She could see that the ceiling was off and there was nothing between herself and the sky, dark and still with an ocean of endless stars.

A sound started to filter through the still night air. It was faint, far away, like something under water or scrambled code across telephone wires.

Then it became clearer, louder.

She tried to move again. *I must find James.*

Then the noise was upon her; shouts, bells, engines, pumps, whistles, horns.

She called out, a broken, feeble sound. Not like her own voice at all. She started to push herself up but the pain in her back was excruciating. Captain Hadley's voice came into her head. *Every second counts. Get yourself out of there.* She may well have been talking about the aftermath of a plane crash, but it was good advice, Bit by bit she rolled herself over, the debris sliding off her. She rested on all fours with her head hanging down, her hair wet though and her clothes shredded.

The whistles and shouts were close by. Slowly, she managed to haul herself up, leaning gingerly on the crumbling walls.

Below and between the gaps in the walls, she could see shadows and torches flashing across the ground. She called towards the mountain of rubble below. Her ankle buckling under her.

'Please, over here!' The rain started to pour, drenching her whole body. 'Please! It's my friend! HELP!'

'Okay Miss. We're here. What's your name.' A man in a uniform flashed his torch towards her.

She blinked into the light. 'Verona, but it's my friend that I'm worried about.' She shivered in the cold night air. 'His name is James…. James Ford. Please hurry!'

The voices and the sound of the whistles swam around in her head.

'Mr Ford…. Mr James Ford...Sir…..... Can you hear us?'

'James, JAMES!'

'V…VERONA! Wake up dear! Wake up!' Mrs Buchanan felt her skin. It was cold even though the fire was blazing in the grate.

She came too, her heart racing.

'Here I have another blanket for you.'

'Oh…. thank you…. I'm so sorry.' She dropped her head and tears started to fall. 'You see they did find him. They had to dig him out.' She put her head in her hands.

'You've had an awful shock my dear.' Her host said kindly, gently tucking the blankets in around her.

'Drink your tea. Then you must rest.'

Chapter Twelve

It was a cold, February morning. Starlings strummed chords on the wires and snow was starting to blow, drifting into banks, along the narrow lanes.

Both the Officers Mess and the little cottage were full, scattered with trunks, kit bags and suitcases.

The ATA were on the move.

Brenda was looking forward to the change the most. She had survived the London bombing 'by merciful luck,' having little choice but to stay where she was. She and her dance partner had been amongst the last to leave and when the siren went off, the basement proved to be as good as place as any in which to take shelter.

Unfortunately, their optimism did not last long. Morning soon revealed the extent of the bombings from the night before. Almost half of the hotel had been blasted out. This meant there was a long and painful wait until rescuers could reach them, plus an equally long and treacherous scramble through the piles of rubble, twisted metal and burst water pipes. Brenda was lucky to escape with only a few cuts and bruises.

V was also recovering and had also been lucky in terms of her injuries. She had escaped with some temporary, partial loss of hearing and a twisted ankle, which was now on the mend.

What she hadn't escaped however, was the terror of it all. Her dreams were vivid and distressing and she didn't know how to stop them.

'Maybe you don't need to lovely,' suggested Phyll one morning after she had tossed and turned through another fitful night.

'Perhaps they show how much you need to get out of your system, to talk it over with someone. Would the doc be able to help. I'm no expert, but maybe he would be the best person to speak to?'

V couldn't agree with this suggestion. It went against all the rules drummed into her as a child.

'Absolutely, out of the question!'

Stiff upper lip and all that.

In the end V decided that the only thing for it was to get airborne again. She couldn't possibly allow herself the luxury of 'mooching' (as she liked to call it). This was the best way to honour the memory of James, her brother and all the others that had lost their lives in this war so far.

'What did happen to your brother?' the Flight Lieutenant had asked on their day out to Lincoln.

They had been walking hand in hand, through the Abortorium, with its winter bare branches and creeping fog. V had not turned to look at him when she replied, but continued to walk, looking straight ahead, down the tree lined path in front of her.

'He was shot down over France.' She replied, trying to sound matter of fact, but in truth feeling a little exposed.

He stopped and pulled her to him. 'I'm sorry,' he whispered.

She let him hold her tight and kiss her gently on the head.

Comforted and comforting, they unfurled from each other and when they did so, he noticed the scrap of silk material in her hand.

'What is it V?'

She uncurled her fingers and it lay flat and limp in the palm of her hand. 'It is from my brother's scarf.'

Gently he closed her hand back around it. 'Come on,' he said gently, 'let's go into the cathedral and light a candle for him.'

She nodded, pushing it back into the warm pocket of her jacket and linking her arm through his added: 'How about we light a candle for them all.'

'All ok my lovely?' Phyll's voice brought her sharply back to the present moment. 'You look a million miles away.'

She shrugged as the memories melted away. 'I'm ok darling.'

'I wish you would let Jane and I help you pack. You look done in. How about I make you a cup of tea? It will pick you up a bit. Looks like you've had another night of it.'

'It wasn't the best and tea would be lovely. I'm absolutely fine with packing though. What would have helped, is if Doc hadn't delayed the start of my training for yet another three weeks.'

'Only to help you get back into the cockpit lovely.'

'Yes well frankly, it's a damned irritation!' she sighed, as she tucked some books into her bag.

'Well look on the bright side. There'll be no Captain Pops, you've graduated anyway and there will be a whole bunch of lovely new people to meet!'

'What about Captain Pops?' Jane appeared, bleary eyed on the landing. She too had spent a fitful night; conversations with Richard Reynolds running repeatedly around in her head.

'Just that she won't be at Broadlands to boss us about. Good grief! You're another one who looks like you've had a night of it!'

'You can say that again!' Jane yawned wearily. ' Is there any tea left in the tin?'

'Yes, but we're down to our last ounce lovely. I was just about to put the kettle on. Good excuse to use it up. Make a big pot Janey.'

'Waste not, want not, remember? An ounce will see us through another week!' Jane smiled through her tetchiness. I'll make us one now and take what's left with us.'

'Leave it to stand darling. I can't bear dish water!' V triumphantly snapped her suitcase shut, using her left hand 'Finished!! Told you I could manage it myself!'

Jane shivered. It was cold in the kitchen and the fire was beginning to dwindle. Phyll had managed to parboil some water, using last night's embers, plus a little extra wood and stoking, but it needed building up again. She threw in a log and poked the crackling timbers, warming her hands as she did so.

Was it really their last day? She could barely believe it. Even less believable was the conversation between herself and Richard the night before.

But the letter in her pocket proved otherwise.

'I'd like to tell you why I left the RAF.' He had told her the previous Friday afternoon. She had just landed and he had been waiting for her, watching as she had taxied in to stop.

'Richard!,' she exclaimed, unbuckling her helmet. 'What are you doing here? I thought you were in Cambridge today?'

'That **was** the plan.' He seemed a little flushed, agitated, even a little shy. 'But I've decided to go tomorrow instead. I just couldn't have you going without saying goodbye properly.'

'But we have Richard. Last time we met - remember?'

They walked shoulder to shoulder over the tarmac and onto the grass beyond. 'We've already said we'll keep in touch.' She swung her helmet by her side. It felt good that he seemed to want to see her again. In truth she felt a little elated.

'We did.. But I feel...that perhaps...being friends and all that...well.... there are things you should know.'

'Things - Richard?'

'Meet me at The Fox and Crown later?'

She stopped 'You're being mysterious. Now I feel a little nervous!'

'No need,' he smiled, turning to face her and picking up her hands in his. 'About Eight-if that's ok with you?'

She nodded slowly, studying his face.

'Ok. Richard. Eight is it.'

***

Later that evening, he told her his story. She listened, watching as the flames from the log fire flushed his cheeks. His hands around a glass of whisky.

He had been flying Hurricanes in '39 and was section leader. A new pilot had just joined the Squadron.

'He was eighteen - just a boy. The weather was atrocious. We had climbed through the clouds, but the group couldn't rely on their instruments and they were following my wingtips. When we eventually burst through there were enemy fighters on our tail. We tried climbing again, but there was a volley of fire and I could see the boy behind me grappling for control, with fire in the cockpit and smoke streaming from his tail.'

'That must have been hellish.'

'The thing is, I didn't see if he manged to bail out. My own aircraft was shot through and when smoke started to come from the nose of it, I had to…' He stopped.

'Bail out yourself?'

'I had to.'

'Of course. What else could you do?'

'I was the Section leader. I was responsible for him.' He swallowed hard and she instinctively laid her hand upon his. 'His mother came to see me. She wanted to know everything - whether there was a chance he could have bailed out too.'

'You did everything you could. Hurricanes are brilliant planes, but we both know there is little space between the fuselage, the engine and the pilot. A jet of flame can shoot through in a minute.' She paused. 'Is this why you went back to Cambridge?'

He nodded: 'To see if there was another way to design things; to help pilots buy more time to get out. You see the boy might have …' His voice trailed off.

'Bailed out too? *No* Richard,' she said firmly, 'you did absolutely the right thing. It was the ***only*** thing you could have done.'

Up to this point, he had been staring ahead; recalling those memories, his jaw set stiffly with the strain of it all. When he had finished, he turned to look at her and could see that had been studying him, her expression frank and without judgment.

For the first time he felt a weight lift from his shoulders. He took a deep breath, his jaw softening and his shoulders relaxing.

'I've never told this to anyone before.'

'Then I'm happy that you have told me. Look, we all

need to keep a rational head. All we can do is try our best in any given situation. It's all we can ever do.'

'You're right.' He touched her face softly..'

'Exactly.'

'Thank you for listening. I'm going to miss you Jane Harrison.' He hesitated for a moment and then continued: 'I didn't just invite you here to explain things a little.'

'You didn't?'

'No, I wanted to give you something.'

He reached inside his jacket pocket, drawing out a small white envelope.

'This is for you.' He pressed it into her hand. It had her name written neatly across the front.

'It's just a few words to say thank you; for helping me, for bringing me out of my shell,' he smiled and the crease between his brow softened. 'Read it, but not here, not tonight.'

She looked at him inquiringly, then nodded and in that moment and without hesitation, he lifted her chin and kissed her; softly at first and then with a passion like he would never have this moment again.

Later that evening they strolled back to the cottage, arm in arm. The sky was clear, and she wished that this moment could last forever.

'I'm going to miss you when you leave,' he whispered as they reached the gate.

'The same, so very much.'

He pulled her close. 'Who's the girl with a room all to herself?' he whispered.

'That would be me.'

They didn't need to talk. Jane pushed at the heavy oak door and they climbed the box stairs as quietly as they could.

***

The compartments were full by the time the train steamed out of the station and included a large and noisy group of children on their way back to the city after some temporary evacuation amongst the fields and villages of rural Lincolnshire.

There was barely a space amidst the plush but faded scarlet seats.

V was asleep, lulled by sips of brandy for the pain. Phyll was writing to Eddie, Brenda and Maria were reading by the dim lamp that illuminated the carriage and Hattie was 'resting her lids' as she liked to describe it.

Jane stared out of the window. She barely heard the soft squeal of the machinery propelling them down the tracks. Her thoughts were entirely on Richard, his letter and on the words which she had read over and over again

She rustled in her bag to retrieve it and once again she unfolded the thin creased notepaper, savouring every word:

Dearest Jane,

I want to say so much, but I'm awkward with words and so I'll try to get to the heart of the matter.

There is something so wonderful about you. When I see you it feels like I am coming home. Before you, there were times when I felt nothing but gloomy and low. Then you came along, and my life brightened and the sun came out.

I have never loved a woman as I love you. Nothing before can compare to the way my heart beats now.

I hope you feel the same and I'll be here, waiting at Mayfield, for when you get back.

That's if you'll have me.

Richard

Jane's heart pounded in her chest. She could never have imagined that he ever could or would write a letter such as this. These were not '*awkwar*d' words, but poetic, heartfelt and sincere.

She read and re-read them and knew exactly how ***she*** felt and it seemed incredible to her, that she could feel this way for she was sure she had not had such feelings before. In fact she had never been more sure of herself. She had not stopped smiling these past few weeks.

She kissed the letter, opened her book and tucked it between the pages. Outside, she could see that the snow was starting to fall, her eyes following the wet spots splattering against the windows. They slid down and melted away. Soon the fields would be covered in another blanket of snow.

He loves me. She felt a glow of pleasure; a wonderful, light joyous feeling.

A sudden squeal of brakes and a shout from Maria and she was soon brought to her senses.

'Come on everybody! Next stop is us! *Estupendo* !'

Phyll snapped shut her book and peered through the smoky windows. She could see the glint of wings in the sky. 'Aircraft dead ahead. Yes we must be in the right place!'

Jane looked out. She could see specks in the distance, flying back to the shelter of the aerodrome. They shimmered through the snowy clouds.

Pulling herself together, she gave V a gentle nudge.

'Wake up sleepy head. We're rolling into the station. Look! *B R O A D L A N D S*! Time for the next chapter.'

Chapter Thirteen
Broadlands Aerodrome, Oxfordshire

Ferry Pool 6a had all been billeted to the Mess, with rooms located on the lower floor.

'It's like school all over again,' said V as she unpacked her bags and popped her toothbrush in its glass.

'Except there are boys here,' called Brenda, from her room.

'Some very nice boys!' agreed Maria.

'Have you seen my hairbrush Phyll?' Jane popped her head around the door. 'Wow, are you alright?'

Phyll was sitting on the bed clutching a letter. It had been waiting for her at reception when they arrived.

'It's from Eddie. Her eyes were red and puffy. 'Bad news I'm afraid.'

'Why what's happened? Is he ok?' Jane immediately came in and sat beside her.

'Here.' Phyll passed her the letter. 'He's been injured.'

Jane noted the date; it was already three weeks old.

My dearest darling Ferry Pool Girl,

I am sorry for the long delay in writing. Now please don't be alarmed; I'm in hospital. I've had a bit of a bump, but I'm quite ok.

Bad luck on me. I took a swipe and the Spit flipped. The next thing I knew I was pulling on the rip cord and falling into the water. I don't remember anything else except waking up in a hospital bed.

I'm sure I'll be back to my old self in no time. All arms and legs are fully operational. I was damned lucky. They fished me out in the nick of time.

I would love to see you. You're a tenacious old thing and I know you will find out where I am.

Yours,

Eddie

Jane put her arm around her friend. 'You're bound to worry.'

'Yep.'

'But Phyll, think about how lucky he's been. He seems to have escaped with relatively few injuries.'

'He'll be playing it down lovely.'

'Well that maybe true but look on the bright side. He seemed to have escaped pretty much unscathed *and* he's alive!'

'I'm trying to look at it that way, but isn't just a matter of time?'

'Now stop that Phyllis Edwards! Eddie wouldn't want you talking like this!'

Phyll smiled weakly. 'I suppose not.'

'Besides, you have a job to do. We need some intel on his whereabouts. He may be closer than you think.'

News travelled quickly and it wasn't long before Phyll had been granted a day's leave to take the journey to St Ambrose where Eddie had been located.

She awoke early to pack a bag with some warm clothes. Her plan was to take the bus, but she has researched the trip and there was a mile or so walk from the last stop to the hospital. She needed to be prepared because the weather was windy and cold. She was still packing when Jane stuck her head around the door.

'Now no arguments now because I'm coming with you. Young Tommy Mitchell's also there and I would love to see how he's doing.'

'Ah the young man we helped at Mayfield. Great idea, thanks Jane, I'd really like that. But how will you clear it with the captain?'

'I've already done that. She has swopped rotas around. We can go together.'

Phyll breathed a sigh of relief. She would be glad of the company. 'That's settled then. I've even saved my chocolate ration.'

***

The Convent turned hospital was a good hour's bus journey from Broadlands and was punctuated by many stops and starts.

'It's probably not that far-just feels like it. It seems to be stopping at every farm and village!'

Phyll was right to pack extra woollens. Strong winds blew clouds across the sky and bent the elms that lined the fields along the way and the final stretch of the journey was a chilly one.

St Ambrose was a large austere Victorian convent, with turrets, tree filled grounds and sweeping steps leading up to the door.

Inside and away from the wind, it was peaceful with their footsteps echoing around the vast circular hall.

'Gosh what a place!' Jane looked around. There was a sweeping staircase with a set of wooden chairs placed in a row against the wall. There was a long counter too and a small statue of *Our Lady at Lourdes* at the far end of it.

'It's very grand.' Phyll felt like whispering. 'Requisitioned by the looks of it.'

'And for that we are most grateful!' A nursing sister appeared from out one of the side hallways. She wore a crisp, yellow uniform, starched and stiff.

'Morning my dears. You must be the two young ladies from Broadlands. I believe we spoke on the phone some time ago.' She approached them, warmly. 'I'm Sister Mary Angela,' she said taking a notebook from her pocket. 'Now let me see, who are you here for Aircraftsman Tommy Mitchell and Flight Lieutenant Eddie Edwards.'

'We are,' they answered together.

'We were wondering if we could see them separately, but at the same time?' asked Phyll tentatively.

'Of course! That is easy to arrange. Who's to see the Flight Lieutenant?'

'That will be me Ma'am.'

'Then you come with me.' She went over the counter and rang the bell. A young lady appeared from a room at the back of the counter.

'Miss Smith, could you kindly take this young lady to see Tommy Mitchell - Ward 4.'

The lady behind reception nodded as she opened the hinged flap on the desk and made her way through to the front.

'This way please Ma'am.'

***

Eddie opened his eyes. The impact of hitting the water had caused him to go into shock. He still felt a bit out of it.

'Is that you my love?'

'Oh Eddie. Are you all right? I was so worried.'

Phyll hugged and kissed him. He looked pale and drawn.

'I am now I've seen you!'

She drew the curtains a little around his bed.

'My Eddie,' she said putting her arms around his neck. 'Are you badly injured?'

'No not really at all. My back took a battering, but nothing's broken.'

'Thank goodness that's all it is. I love you so much Eddie Edwards. I want you home in one piece. We still have the decorating to do on the flat remember!'

Eddie grimaced as he tried to pull himself up a little.

'I keep thinking we should give that up love. God knows when this crazy war will end!'

'Now don't talk like that. We're keeping it because it *will end* and then we'll be busy getting it just the way we want it.'

'That's true, but I keep thinking about the farm too Phyll and all the work mother has to do now the boys have joined up.'

'I know and it will be hard for her, but my Uncle Hugh has offered to help, plus Cousin Bronwyn has written to say she can live in for a while. Remember too, there's the local land army who can spare an extra day a week.'

He brightened a little. 'Yes, that will definitely help things. That's really good of Bronwyn.'

'Anyway, what happened lovely? Were you showing off?'

He tried to sit up again, but his back was still tender.

'Ouch! I'm feeling it Phyll! Not showing off,' he smiled weakly. 'It was just bad luck that's all. We'd been sent to intercept some raiders heading for the ports. I spotted a

Messerschmitt and managed to fire a burst. I then found myself in pursuit of a Heinkel, but it was too far away. I was caught on the tail. That's pretty much it.'

He couldn't tell her how lucky he'd been to survive that night.

'Well, you're here and that's all that matters.' She lowered her voice and whispered. 'I thought you were being sent overseas?'

He looked about and pulled her to him. 'Day sorties to France for the moment. But that's about to change.'

They held onto each other, until a nurse came and drew the curtains back with visiting time over.

***

'Visitor for you Sir!' Jane had followed the young desk clerk through the long, white-washed corridors, right to the far end of the hospital.

The young man was propped up with pillows at the end of a long ward. He had a magazine that someone had given him and was eating an apple.

He grinned shyly: 'Sir? I've not been called that before.'

The desk clerk laughed and nodded.

'Best get used to it then. This nice lady here has been telling me how brave you've been.'

He grinned. 'They told me you were coming.'

'Cadet Harrison,' she said introducing herself. 'It's good to see you're on the mend.'

'I've been told you saved my life.'

Jane pulled a chair up next to him. 'We just kept you going until help arrived.'

His smiled faded a little and he dropped his head.

'I don't remember much about it.' He let out a deep sigh and shook his head. 'There were just these sirens and flashes of very bright light.'

Tears started to roll down his cheeks.

'Tommy,' Jane leaned forward and held his hand. 'Try not to think about it? You're safe now.'

She reached inside her bag. 'Here, look, I've bought something for you - chocolate, a month's supply. I've been saving it up.'

His face brightened. 'Thank you. That's grand.' He took the bar and broke off a square.

'One for you and one for me.'

Chapter Fourteen

The Ops room at Broadlands was filling up. News had spread that ships were being attacked in the Channel and every fighter was being scrambled to protect them. The need for new or repaired aircraft was inexhaustible and the demands on the ATA for deliveries were increasing every day. As a consequence, the friends were rapidly progressing through a range of aircraft; now embarking on a conversion course for Class 3s.

There was no question that life for the ATA had stepped up a pace; there were days when it wasn't uncommon to do three, even four transfers; with early starts and even later finishes and it was inevitable that with an increase in flying there came an increase in risk.

Hattie Sykes was the first to run into trouble. She had picked up a chit for a Spitfire and was on her way back from the factory when she got caught in a blanket of fog, so thick, that she could barely see the nose of the plane in front of her. Immediately she thought of the barrage balloons; large, tethered inflatables used to defend ground targets against aircraft attack and mainly situated around the coast. She was barely out of Southampton and was in that area. She looked at her compass and hoped that by flying directly northeast, she could avoid them.

She had no idea why her compass had decided to stop working that day. How can you explain these things when it could have been any other much brighter, clearer day?

She flew for a while in a sickening soup of grey mist. She could barely see anything, not even the wings to either side of the plane. Hattie was not a girl given to panic, but she was feeling increasingly concerned. Any manner of danger presented itself now; stray planes (either side), anti-aircraft guns and of course the barrage balloons.

In hindsight it all happened so quickly.

Firstly, there was a dull, sickening sound and a jolt that came upon her so fast, that she barely realised what was happening. For a while, the aircraft rocked violently backwards and forward, caught in the ties of the barrage balloon; the sound of metal upon metal as a cable sliced into a wing. Her assessment was immediate. No broken bones, no lacerations; by some almighty stroke of luck the windshield had held intact.

She sat very still, barely daring to breathe. Any movement on her part could knock this thing out of the sky. She needed to bail out and NOW! But, what of the Spit? It would surely fall and what would it fall on? Who was beneath her? She felt sick. *Damn! No radio, no maydays.* This was not good. She grappled with her harness and the engine coughed to a stall.

For a while all was still, except for the creaking of the metal ties and the whistle of the wind outside. It felt like she was suspended in time.

But then the clock started ticking again.

She started to fumble with the harness, her breath coming in short bursts. As she did so, she felt a strange sensation. The aircraft was tipping, it started to creak and slide. Just a little at first and then a jolt and then it slid some more, tipping backwards.

Ok. You're going to have to do this in one movement and you are going to have to do it now!

There was another jolt and a screech of metal. With one almighty heave she unclipped her harness and wrenched the hatch. There was no risk of hitting the tail or stabilisers on exit as it was already tipping at an alarming angle.

For a while all she could hear was the wind as it rushed past her ears as she fell and tumbled. Then there was the 'whoosh' of her parachute as it billowed open and started the drag, swinging her this way and that until eventually, she reached the ground with a bump and a crack of her ankle.

A moment later and the machine plummeted after her, descending at sickening speed and landing with an almighty explosion into the middle of a highway. It was soon engulfed in an orange glow; parts scattered to the wind. A van out for deliveries, screeched to a juddering stop, its driver jumping out and running away back down the road, not stopping until he came across the pilot lying on her side wedged between a hedge and a ditch.

'She was *so* lucky.' exclaimed Jane on hearing the news. Thank god, it was just a broken ankle. What will happen to her? Where is she now?'

'On her way home to convalesce, but she'll be back,' assured the Ground Instructor. 'That girl's made of strong stuff.'

It was bad news for Brenda too. News came through that her sister, a nurse, had been killed in a raid on a hospital in the city. The building had received a direct hit with many casualties. Brenda was sent home on compassionate leave and during that time she helped with the clean-up, supporting other grieving families.

It was the only way she could find some resolution.

Then other women started to arrive at the Ferry Pool, joining from other stations around the country. There were those on conversion courses, those who needed to change stations for personal reasons and those who were just starting out, fresh faced and full of energy.

Of the original group only Maria, V, Phyll and Jane remained.

***

'Morning everybody!' greeted the Flight Officer, early one May morning. 'Chits are ready. Lots of them today. Where's Bowes Hudson?'

V burst in, after another restless night. She had been cleared fit for work for some weeks now and at first felt ok; but then the clouds came over and the memories came back and for a while her nights were haunted by vivid and unsettling dreams.

'Here Ma'am!' she proclaimed breathlessly.

'Overslept again? Now come on, BH, the medics thinks

you're up to it. I think you're up to it. Now what do you think?'

'She might feel better if she put a little lippy on!' teased Phyll. 'Come on V, standards are slipping. Where's that girl that would never fly unless she looked like a movie star.'

'Absent without leave at the moment.'

'Then fetch her back again lovely!'

'Do not worry Verona, I have a beautiful colour here!' Maria dug in her flying suit pocket.

V took it and turned the little shell around in her hand.

'It's the texture of candle wax!'

'Come on put some on!' Maria handed her a small compact.

'Okay I give in!' She pulled the waxy red colour around her lips.

'Now you're talking.' Phyll gave her a friendly shove. 'That's more like it.'

The Flight Instructor coughed and looked around.

'Bowes Hudson, you have Spit pick-ups today. Two of them, plus a spare parts collection. Fancy a Mustang too?'

'Absolutely Sir!'

'Excellent. Check your pilot's notes!'

V slipped the orders into her boot and made her way across to the Dispersal Room, where she carried out the usual weather checks. She headed towards the Avro taxi and looked at the chits. First on the list was a trip to the factory for a Kenley drop off. The rest she could check out later. Quite a day. She caught her reflection in the aircraft's window, the red lipstick bright in her monochrome reflection.

Familiar feelings of frustration and restlessness swept over her again.

Good, she thought. *It's ok to feel like this. Better than feeling as flat as the fields round here.*

'Harrison?'

'Ma'am'

'Chits here for the following: factory drop off for Lyneham. Repeat twice. Then back to pick up a Typhoon for drop off at Mayfield.'

Jane's heart skipped a beat. *Mayfield? This couldn't be better. She could see Richard-even if it were only for an hour or two.*

She took the chits and held them tightly in her hand.

***

V had exchanged her first chit for a refurbished Spit and wasted no time taxiing down the runway for a take-off to Kenley. She loved flying this aircraft. It could be a little skittish and hard to manage on the ground, but once in the air-well nothing could beat it and it was times like these that she thought of James. He had loved this little plane.

The aerodrome came into view, it was easy to spot and heavily cratered. It had obviously taken quite a pounding.

She approached suddenly remembering her instructions from Phyll:

'Could you ask if Eddie's there? I haven't heard from him for ages.'

'I'll try.'

'Please do.' Phyll kissed a letter and gave it to her friend. 'And fly safely V. You've had a lot on your mind lately.'

'Of course. My red lippy's on! You watch me!'

V had a wonderful fight. It almost felt like she had grown wings of her own, soaring through the sky, smoothly and effortlessly Eventually, she came to taxi in, bumping and jumping over the holes in the tarmac.

There was a group of pilots on the grass waiting to be scrambled. They waved as she climbed out of the cockpit and she called back.

She was beginning to recognise all of them.

'V! Over here!' They called.

'How about a round of cricket!'

'Or a smoke?'

'I'll take that,' laughed V.

She sat with them, smoked, drank weak tea and asked after Eddie Edwards.

'He's not here,' replied an airman lolling back, exhausted in his deckchair. 'That squadron has long gone.'

'Any ideas where to? His wife is out of her mind with worry.'

'Well keep it under your hat old girl, but rumour has it they may be a *long way* overseas - somewhere warm. Of course, that may not be true.'

V jumped up. 'Thanks for that.' She understood that any other rumours might be careless.

'Spare parts are ready for you now Ma'am!' shouted one of the ground crew.

The pilot smiled. 'Come back and see us.'

'You can count on it! Goodbye and don't do anything I wouldn't do!'

She ran to the plane and jumped onto the wing, settling herself into the cockpit. One of the ground crew called up and rested his hand on the fuselage.

'Nothing much wrong with her. Just needs the factory to tweak a few things. Here's the itinerary. Perfectly safe to fly.'

V looked at it. It was just superficial stuff, nothing that wouldn't take long to fix. 'Ok that's fine,' she said running through the pre-flight checks.

She looked about her. Kenley had suffered so much damage and had so little to protect it. They'll be back, she thought. How much more could these boys take? The pilots were exhausted, half-crazy through lack of sleep. Many were starting to take risks too, games to keep them alert and awake.

Games to numb the pain.

Why wouldn't you when your friends were being shot down?

A couple of pilots were 'horsing' around, looping the loop above the aerodrome, while the others kept tally on the ground.

For a while V watched them swoop and dive above her.

Blow it! 'Contact!' She called.

She started the engine and taxied until she could feel the torque at full power. Then she eased the stick forward to raise the tail, lifting the plane into the air.

Chapter Fifteen

Jane had completed her deliveries to Lyneham and by early afternoon, she was flying east to Mayfield. The fields were filled with all manner of new life and the promise of summer to come. It was a beautiful day and an odd juxtaposition between war and peace.

She flew cautiously, because she not familiar with the Typhoon. It had taken her some time to carry out the pre-flight checks, even with the help of the pilot's notes. Diligently, she checked her navigation instruments and remembered her training. Stay within sight of the ground, use the maps, compass and watch.

The open skies and the peace of the cockpit cocooned her and her thoughts turned to Richard. They had exchanged long loving letters to each other, always taking care with news and locations.

She couldn't wait to see him again. It would be such a surprise after all these months.

The landing strip at Mayfield came into view. '*It looks different. There's a new runway.*' She approached slowly; she wasn't taking chances. This aircraft was desperately needed.

She landed well, managing to avoid most of the holes in the tarmac. Once the chocks were in place, she was able to climb out of the cockpit and unbuckle her helmet. A group of pilots were resting on chairs in the grass, waiting for their next instructions.

She waved over: 'How are you all?'

A young man, with a tired face, waved a crumpled newspaper. 'Some of us are still here, holding on by the skin of our teeth!'

Jane nodded and walked over. 'Every day must be hard.'

'Same for everyone. Same for you.' He dug in his pocket and pulled out a battered box. 'Smoke Harrison?'

'Thanks!' she took one from the box and tucked it into her top pocket. 'I'll save it for later. I have a few jobs to do first.'

The young pilot lit his cigarette and nodded. 'See you around.'

She took the path around the perimeter. It was a familiar walk and she smiled at the memory of her first day here. Who would have guessed she would make such wonderful friends on that day or meet the illusive Dr Richard Reynolds.

Ops were busy. She could hear typing, radio operatives and plotters from behind the partition.

A shock of blond hair appeared from behind the hatch. 'Afternoon Ma'am.'

Jane nodded in recognition. 'Delivery for you! 'One sparkling Typhoon, fresh from the factory floor!'

She retrieved the slip of paper from her boot.

'Thank you, Ma'am. That is good news.' The WAAF took the chit and passed her a pen.

Jane scribbled her name.

'Is there anything else I can help you with Ma'am?'

'Actually, there is. I'm looking for Dr Reynolds. Has he been here today?'

'Let's check the signing in book.' The WAAF looked down the page.

'Yes. He signed in at 10am for a meeting, which finished some hours ago. He will most likely be in one of the hangers, or the Mess where he's billeted.'

'The Mess?'

'Yes Ma'am. I believe that's where his accommodation is.'

'I see,' Jane was puzzled. He hadn't mentioned anything about changing billets.

'Would you like me to put a call out Ma'am?'

Jane hesitated. 'No…it's fine. I'll find him. 'Thank you corporal.

She was confused. He hadn't told her he had moved from the Brigadier's house. She looked at her watch; only an hour before the Avro would taxi back to pick her up.

She needed to see him.

She headed off, remembering a short cut to the Mess via a wooded area. Here the path weaved around to the dining room, which could be entered from the side of the building through some French doors.

Inside, china was being laid out. A young girl in a white apron was placing down rows of plates and tumblers, whilst an older one was laying out the cutlery.

They looked up with a start. A figure was standing by the doors, silhouetted against the bright sun and wearing a dust covered flying suit.

'Ma'am?' inquired the older one and then remembering her manners, added: 'May I help you?'

The figure moved into the cool shade of the room and the girls could see how pale she looked; her hair damp, her brow reddened by the indentations of her flying helmet.

'Yes, if you could.' Jane paused and looked around. She suddenly felt a little sick. 'I'm looking for a Dr Reynolds?'

'Dr Reynolds?' repeated the older one. 'He's upstairs Ma'am. Second Floor. Room 2a.' She pointed to the far end of the dining room and to some heavily carpeted stairs.

'Thank you. Most helpful.' Jane nodded, a little amused by their curiosity. She took a deep breath and moved off.

'Mary, would you believe it!' whispered the younger girl excitedly. 'I think she was one of those 'ATTA' girls. You know-like the ones in your magazine!'

The other girl agreed and they stared open mouthed after her, noting that she hesitated before taking the stairs. It was the briefest of moments, but it was clear to see.

'She doesn't look so happy. Do you think there's trouble afoot?'

'Could be, could be,' nodded Mary agreeing. 'After all, he does seem a bit of a rum'un, what with his comings and goings at all times of the day and night!'

***

The stairs were poorly lit and Jane climbed them with some trepidation. The stillness in the day time unnerved her, but she tried to be as quiet as possible; the night bomber crews would still be sleeping.

She found his room, it was at the end of the corridor, next to an aspidistra and a brooding painting of the Somme. She knocked gently. She told herself she was being ridiculous, he had just forgotten to mention changing billets.

'Who is it?' She jumped and her heart skipped a beat. She was about to reply when she stopped.

There was another voice alongside Richard's.

'Tell them we're busy Dicky.'

Jane froze. The voice was young, determined; a woman's voice.

The key started to rattle in the lock and for one moment she considered running, and as far away as possible, all rational thoughts escaping her.

But then Richard's head appeared.

He stared at her, incredulously; her blue eyes, wide with surprise and confusion.

'Jane! I wasn't expecting...'

'Me to drop in?' She answered almost immediately; a touch of irony in her voice. She didn't sound like herself at all.

He stepped quickly into the corridor, pulling the door behind him.

'Look, I know what you must be thinking….'

'Perhaps you don't.' Her voice sounded brittle.

'Let me explain. It's ***not*** what you think. It's complicated Jane. Delicate.'

'Is there a problem Dicky?' came the voice from inside.

'It doesn't sound delicate!'

'Listen, let's go somewhere else. We can talk.' He tried to take her arm, but she brushed it off.

'No need.' She shook her head vigorously and started to back away. 'I was making a delivery and called by on the off chance. You're busy. We'll catch up some other time.'

'Jane please. Give me a chance to explain.' He held out his hands in supplication.

She shook her head. 'No Richard, I have to go.' Tears were coming, she had to get out.

'Please don't!'

She reached the end of the corridor, then stopped, taking a deep breath.

'Goodbye Richard,' she said, turning away from him. She didn't feel like herself at all and with that she left him, staring down the corridor after her.

***

It was Phyll who first noticed that V was missing.

'Where the heck is she? Her bed's not been slept in!'

'Not so loud!' shouted Brenda who had just returned from compassionate leave and was struggling to readjust to the early morning wake up calls. 'She'll have met a fellow.'

'I don't think she's strong enough for that. Her bed has definitely ***not*** been slept in.'

'Who are we talking about?' Jane emerged looking pale and puffy eyed.

'V – there's no sign of her. Wow are you all right? You look awful.'

'I've been better.' she replied wearily, having spent another fitful and tiresome night. Three weeks had passed since seeing Richard and his silence was almost too much to bear.

'Janey?'

'Sorry Phyll, I'm here. Ok, so where exactly is V?' she said pulling her robe about her.

'No idea! She should have completed all drop offs by seven last night.'

Suddenly, Maria appeared breathless at the top of the stairs. She'd been down to check the post and one of the morning crew had caught up with her.

'Bad, BAD news!' She could barely get her words out. 'Terrible news!'

The group huddled together in the corridor.

'What is it Maria?,' Jane held her hand. She was shaking.

'It's V. She's had a crash!'

There was exclamations of shock all round.

'Oh my lord!' Phyll gasped. 'Is she ok?'

'They say she's alive but injured.

'Oh mercy,' Brenda shook her head. 'What happened?'

'She attempted *Rollo bajo*.'

'A low roll? Too low by the sounds of it. Poor V, did they say where they've taken her? Perhaps it's St Ambrose where Eddie is.' Phyll was already heading back to her room to retrieve her bag.

'Where are you off to?' Jane called after her.

'Going to see her lovely/

'No trains running today,' Brenda raised her hands in despair. 'Lines out of service. Debris on the track at Littlehampton.'

Jane nodded. 'No buses either. They are still trying to make safe the bomb dropped onto the road at Smithorpe.'

'Well, we must get there **somehow**.' Phyll started to stuff the bag with some necessities. 'I can cycle. It will probably only take a couple of hours.'

'So, we'll need two bicycles, because I'm coming.' Jane was already pulling her plimsolls on.

'You can't. It's not your rest day.'

'I'll swop,' volunteered Maria, 'I'm sure the captain will be fine about it.'

Phyll nodded. She would be glad of the company. 'Right, that's sorted then. Come on Janey. Grab your things.'

***

'Two bike, two repair kits. Return first thing in the morning. Sign here please.'

The sergeant passed over the necessary paperwork and went to fetch them from the back of the building.

'Here you go, sturdy things these. They should get you there no problem!'

'Thanks!' Phyll tucked her trousers into the clips and took the bicycle from him..

'If you give me a minute, I can draw you a map, one that should avoid road closures. I come from these parts.'

'That would be useful. Thanks!' Phyll started to wheel around in circles.

'Hey wait for me! Short legs remember!' Jane hopped on and off, moving the seat into a comfortable position. 'Okay that's better. How many miles did you say it was?'

Phyll pushed herself off, wheels wobbling and crunching over the gravel. 'About ten!'

'Here you go.' The sergeant passed Phyll a hastily drawn map. 'It may take a bit longer this way, but at least you won't have to turn back on yourself!'

'Great, thanks!' Phyll tucked it into her jacket pocket and started to pedal across the tarmac and up towards the Guard Room.

Jane followed and they pedalled out of the camp, the spokes ticking like a clock. The sun had already risen and it was warm and bright for May. Trees were blossoming beside hedgerows and the birds were in full song.

V's accident had brought Jane to her senses. She must put the recent events with Richard into perspective. *Best,* she thought, *not to think about it.*

'But maybe there ***was*** a straightforward explanation,' pointed out Phyll along the way. 'Besides, war can do strange things to people.'

Jane shook her head. 'Having someone in your room like that can only mean one thing.'

'Not necessarily.' Phyll rang her bell as they approached a corner. 'The woman could have been there for any number of reasons.'

'Only one in my book! All those letters promising this and that! Watch out Phyll, horses ahead!'

They dismounted. The lane was narrow and it had turned into a single passing. They leaned into the hedge as a girl in khaki overalls passed by. She was leading two horses, both pulling a cart. She nodded at them wearily, her face streaked with mud.

'What would we do without the land army eh?' Phyll climbed back onto her bicycle as she watched them disappear down the lane.

'Agree! What a blessing they've been.'

'Come on Janey! Let's see if we can do the rest of the journey in one stretch!' Phyll started to pedal off.

Jane laughed. She felt better. The warm spring breeze, plus Phyll's company, was wearing down the shock from the previous few weeks.

Captain Pops Hadley stood in the dispersal room. A new

wave of pilots had been briefed and she and a colleague were clearing away.

'News on the grapevine is that Bowes Hudson bought it at Kenners!'

The captain stopped short. 'Bought it?'

'Well brought it upon herself ……low rolling, dropped the wing...BOOM! Injured, not dead.'

The captain looked perplexed and leaned heavily on her stick.

'Damned good pilot-probably the best we had. Her delivery rate was second to none, but she was...how can I put it?'

'Up herself?'

'Quite so.'

The captain picked up the chalk and started to pack it away. 'How badly injured is she? Any reports?'

'Pretty bad.' Her colleague lit himself a cigarette. Casualties were a daily occurrence. *Pilots as young as seventeen, minimal training, lambs to the slaughter.* 'Amputation job, I think.'

'Lord!' The captain shifted her weight. The pain in her leg had been an agitation these last few weeks.

'Poor blighter.'

Chapter Sixteen

Flight Lieutenant Eddie Edwards was exhausted. Flying over France was fraught with danger. Every day young men set out, full of bravado and single minded determination. Every day there were those that did not return.

It was hard to get close to anyone.

Orders changed rapidly and there were rumours of relocation. News came through that things were hotting up in Malta and there was barely a moment to catch breath. One night he had been tucked up in bed having survived another sortie; the next he had been woken up at some god forsaken hour and told to report ASAP to HQ. What was left of his Squadron was on the move. First, to Gibraltar, for an overnight stop, and then onwards to Malta where they were straight into action.

'We're under constant bombardment!' said the Group Captain. 'We're a fly in the ointment. The whole of the South Med to El Alemain is occupied, so they're gunning for us.'

There was no let up. The island was under siege. Food was in short supply and it was emergency rations and hard, stale biscuits for everyone. Accommodation was basic too. Eddie slept fitfully that first night. His barrack bed was as hard as nails and when he awoke, there were bugs crawling all over him. Even the nets couldn't keep them away.

'I'm putting you on reconnaissance Harrison,' said his Squadron Leader who had assembled them for briefing. 'You and Sammy Butler. You can fly out in pairs.'

'Yes, Sir.'

'You'll be on Spits. They're unarmed for altitude. You need to keep an eye out on supply convoys and help protect the Navy. It's their ships that are keeping us topped with fuel.'

Eddie learnt quickly. A rearwards-facing camera could overcome some of the jitter from sideways movement, and low-level photography benefitted from an almost side-ways camera view. Most of their work would need to be done at high altitude.

Each day was an attack on the senses. The islanders were forced to spend much of their time in caves and tunnels to shelter from the incessant and long-lasting air attacks. The sound of anti-aircraft guns, going off like firecrackers, seemed to be a constant and daily raids and dive bombing was taking their toll. The desperate need to dig underground shelters through the rock became increasingly urgent. Convoys bound for Malta were suffering heavy losses. It was a battle to keep morale up.

Eddie felt he was losing it every day.

***

'I have to take your bandages off,' said the young woman placing a lantern down beside the waking man. It was dark outside, and Gerald Harrison wondered what time it was.

'The air must get to your wounds.'

He watched as she gently unravelled the long strings of material from his chest.

'It is much better. Yes, I am pleased with that.'

'Thank you, Claudette. How can I ever repay you. You have saved my life. Of that I am sure.'

'No need for thank you,' she said smiling. 'We do what we can, and you have fought hard to get well again.'

She helped him up. He was shaky on his feet and his head span.

'We must go into the house. You will be more comfortable there and I'm expecting a visitor. Take your time now!'

He descended the ladder carefully but the pain in his chest made him wretch.

She let him lean on her as they crossed the courtyard to the farmhouse door. The building was large and crumbling, with peeling paint and ivy twisting up the walls. Shutters hung off their hinges and the door was warped. She had to push hard in order to open it.

'I can repair that,' he said weakly, as she helped him through the door.

'Merci…but no! It's nothing I can't fix! Here, come and sit by the fire.' She pointed to a large wooden chair and passed him a blanket. 'You must stay warm.'

There was a knock on the door. It was nearly midnight. He froze. She looked at him with a finger to her mouth.

'Ssh!'

Then came another knock. Three loud bangs. Claudette stood up. 'That will be Pierre.'

The stranger entered, a serious young man with a thick jumper and spectacles. He kissed Claudette on both cheeks. She liked him, the injured pilot could see that.

'Pierre.'

'Claudette. It is good to see you. I hope you are well.'

'Come in, sit down. Let me get something for you to eat.'

She cut bread and gave him some cheese which she'd fetched from a square of muslin.

'From Esme, the goat.'

He nodded and took a drink. 'Merci Claudette.' He reached inside his jacket and passed Harrison a packet across the table.

'Here are your papers. You are Basile Martinez, Claudette's Uncle from Avignon. You cannot speak. You have been traumatised by a bombing raid, during which you lost your wife.'

The pilot looked inside the packet and nodded.

'Merci.'

'There are some tickets in there. They are for a train journey - Antwerp to Brussels. You will be going soon.' He broke off some bread.

'How will I get to Antwerp?'

'Claudette will take you by train to the station, from where you will be met by a guide.'

He drank the rest of his wine. 'We can help you get back to England, but you *must* stick to your story and to your new identity. Anything less will place Claudette's life in danger.'

The girl blushed and looked away.

The young man finished his wine and took his last bite of bread. 'Au revoir Claudette. Stay safe.'

She nodded. 'Pierre.'

'Thank you, Monsieur. Thank you very much.' Harrison attempted to stand, but the man signalled for him to stay where he was.

When he left. Claudette bolted the door. 'He is a good man. He has risked his life so many times.'

'Yes, I see that.' He looked at her, not much younger than his own daughter. He felt an ache in his heart. 'Why do you do it Claudette? Why do you risk your life in this way?'

'I am part of the Resistance, fighting against the Occupation. We provide the Allies with intelligence; assist the escape of Allied airmen We do what we can. Pierre is my contact. He gets the papers, ID, the resources we need.'

'*We* need?'

'There are many of us. My parents too. They were good people.'

'You say they *were* good people? Where are they now?'

She turned away from him and poked the fire.

'They were taken. They were caught hiding some of your compatriots.'

'Oh no Claudette. I'm sorry.'

'You have nothing to feel sorry for.'

'Do you know *where* they were taken?'

'Je ne sais pas.' She shook her head sadly. 'You see there are many tunnels and many paths, in which to disappear.'

Chapter Seventeen

V could not remember how long she had drifted in and out of sleep. Nurses came and went, checking drips and taking pulses; their voices seemed muffled and faraway.

'Doctor's on his way,' said the nurse once she came too. 'Let's get you sorted shall we, make you comfortable.'

She tried to speak but her throat was dry and the figure of the nurse seemed to float around before her.

'Here I'll prop you up. Have a sip of water.'

Pillows were plumped and blankets turned down.

'There, you look more comfortable.' The nurse stood back satisfied.

A doctor appeared, looking at his notes. 'Morning Officer. How are you feeling?'

Her voice was barely audible. 'Terrible.'

He nodded understandingly and reached for a clipboard at the end of the bed.

'What's happened?' she asked weakly.

'You've been in a crash. You attempted a roll, but it didn't come off.'

'Oh, Lord!' She shut her eyes.' Of course, it was all coming back: the take-off, the attempt at a 360, the wing clipping the ground, the screaming of metal on tarmac. 'Damned stupid!'

'Sorry I didn't catch that?'

She opened her eyes and tried to focus on his white coat.

'I said I was stupid.'

He pursed his lips. Yes, it had been reckless, but she didn't need to hear that now. Besides, many were still taking those risks. War had that strange effect on people. He looked down at his papers. 'I imagine you'll want it straight?'

She nodded, wishing she didn't have to.

'You've had a nasty bump to the head. It looks ok, but we need to monitor it. You also have a small fracture to the ankle, plus cuts, bruises that sort of thing.'

He paused. These conversations were always difficult, but quite often it was best to deliver the news quickly and kindly.

He cleared his throat. 'I'm sorry, but we also had to carry out some surgery.'

'Surgery?' she repeated weakly.

'You're minus the lower part of your right arm .'

For a moment she did not register, staring blankly at the hazy outline of the doctor in front of her. Then his words started to sink in.

'My arm?'

'We did our best to save it.,' he continued. We pumped you with saline to prevent the blood clotting, but your arm was too badly damaged and we had to take it off.'

She felt the room spin. 'Oh no!'

'I appreciate it's difficult. But, the important thing is you came through.'

'Can I see it? she asked trying to sit up again.

The nurse came over. 'Here, let me help you.' Carefully, she rolled the sheet back. There was no forearm, just a bandaged stump below the right elbow.

'I think I'm going to be sick!'

The nurse tried to hold her up a little. 'Here have a sip of water. You've had a shock.'

She sank her head back into the pillow and closed her eyes. The doctor was talking again but his voice seemed to be fading away.

'Try and get plenty of rest. Once the drips are out see if you can get out of bed and move about as much as possible. The fracture should heal pretty quickly. Keep moving that shoulder too. They'll fix you up with a prosthetic, but not here, you'll need to go to Uxbridge for that.'

A wave of nausea swept over her and sleep threatened to envelop her. Clouds drifted across a blue sky and then she was breaking out of them, pushing into a roll. For one glorious moment she was free; free of war, of loss, of everything and it was just herself and the machine.

***

'We're here!' called Phyll over her shoulder, as they

reached the hospital gates. 'Phew! Mission accomplished!'

'We need to prepare ourselves,' suggested Jane as they climbed the broad sweep of steps. 'V may be very badly injured. We'll have to be..'

'Unflappable?'

'Something like that, yes.'

Phyll linked her arm through Jane's. 'We will be lovely. We're pilots aren't we?'

There was some delay on entering reception. The duty Sister was not happy about such an early visit, but after much conversation with the doctor, they were admitted on the proviso they scrubbed down and borrowed some clean gowns.

V was in a side room and barely recognisable. The night had passed in a haze of morphine and she lay pale and still against the pillow, sheets tucked neatly across her shoulders. There was a bandage around her head and a hooped contraption about her body

'I'm afraid she's drifting in and out of wakefulness,' said the nurse, whispering. 'Try not to stay too long or you'll overtire her.'

Jane moved a chair quietly next to her.

'Poor V,' she whispered. 'She looks so ill.'

The young woman stirred and tried to open her eyes. She could see the outline of two people on either side of her, but the words escaped her.

'Now don't you go fretting yourself lovely. We're just

pleased to see you.' Phyll opened her bag. 'Here, we've bought you something; our chocolate rations for when you're feeling better!'

'We've brought some apples too.' Jane put them on the cabinet next to her bed.

There was the faintest of smiles then her eyes started to shut again.

'Will she be alright?' asked Phyll turning to the nurse.

'She will be if she's strong.'

'She's definitely that.'

'Then that will stand her in good stead. Of course there will be some challenges ahead, getting used to the prosthetic.'

'Prosthetic?'

'She's had an amputation, just below the elbow on her right arm.'

The two women stared with open mouths.

'It will take some getting used to, but she will have help to rehabilitate.'

'Poor V.' Jane shook her head.

'We're right here beside you.' Phyll patted the bed.

'Is you friend a fighter?' asked the nurse.

'Absolutely!' Jane nodded.

'Then she'll be okay.'

She'd seen it repeatedly; mind over matter, the determination to keep going. But it was always a fight and this patient had received not only an amputation, but a head injury too.

Few pilots managed to fly after that.

***

Jane touched the pearls around her neck. Their delicate pinkish sheen resting against her skin.

It was the finishing touch.

She patted her hair. Gone were the chestnut ringlets that would tease their way out of her cap. Now she sported a shorter, more shaped look. She nodded in approval. She'd have a good time whether she felt like it or not. Besides, she was under orders.

Jane had found V awake on her next visit, awake and more alert. She was irritable too.

'It's a good sign,' the nurse had said positively. 'It means she's getting better.'

She was sitting up, supported by several pillows. There was a tray on a table propped over the bed in front of her.

'I simply can't believe I'm going to miss the Ball!'

Jane watched her shakily scoop soup into her mouth.

'Damn it. I've spilt it!'

'Can I help?' Jane passed a cloth.

'No!' said V sharply. 'Sorry but thank you darling. I must practice with this hand, until I get the new one. She tried with the spoon again. 'There that's better. I'm getting the hang of it. Now back to this dance, I'll want to hear all about it!'

'Of course!'

'And absolutely *no* wilting violets.'

Jane laughed 'Yes Ma'am,' she said saluting her.

'Any other orders?'

'I'd like a waltz and foxtrot please!'

Jane took the message back to the girls.

'Ordering us about?,' laughed Phyll, grabbing her sponge bag for the evening's ablutions. 'She is getting stronger! 'I reckon she'll be back in no time!'

'I really hope so.'

'V's made of strong stuff.' Brenda agreed with Phyll.

'Yes, but this time it's different. Remember Fordy? Now she has this to contend with too.'

'She's certainly had a bad time of it. Let's hope she mends quickly. By the way…' said Phyll remembering, 'have you opened your parcel yet?'

Jane laughed. 'No, I'm going to do that now.'

She shut the door and picked up the box resting on the end of her bed. It was covered in brown paper and tied with string. The address was written in her mother's handwriting.

There was much comfort in that.

She ripped off the paper before carefully peeling back the layer of tissue inside the box. Lace rustled amongst the crinkled paper. Carefully she picked up the gown and it dropped to the floor; layers of sumptuous midnight blue lace tied off with a silk ribbon around the waist.

Gently, she slipped it over her head and down against her body. It was beautiful. It was her mother's wedding dress cut, re-tailored and dyed. Tears pricked her eyes. She couldn't thank her enough.

At the bottom of the box lay an envelope. She took out the delicate paper inside; the ink flowing across the page:

Dearest Jane,

I have enclosed a little gift. I hope it fits! I certainly know the colour will suit you and this beautiful piece of material was just lying around!

Darling, I was so sorry to hear of RR. What a disappointment.

*Life has a funny way of working things out. In fact, I can almost hear your father saying that. We know **exactly** what he would say and do! He would give you a big hug you and say he understands how painful things can be. **But,** then he would laugh, brush his sleeves and say, 'dust if off my dear, dust it off!'*

I know these little sayings are probably not much comfort, but remember how much we love you, and how proud we are of you.

Mother x

Jane took a deep breath; the letter was **such** a comfort. Furthermore, her mother had used the collective *'we'*. She was never going to give up on her husband; not until she had absolute proof otherwise.

Jane was sharply reminded of her focus.

She would write another letter to the Ministry tomorrow; *they surely might have some news by now?*

She sighed and picked up her purse. 'Ready!' she called as she shut the door behind her.

***

The room was filling up. A large brick storage unit had been cleared for the dance and spotlights and a mirrored ball had been installed. The glittering globe sent shafts of light like moonlight across the floor and the music serenaded the swaying couples. Whoever could come had tried to come.

Jane remembered Vs instructions; she had completed the foxtrot with Brenda, laughing through the quick and slow steps. Now there was just the waltz left to do. They were just about to move off again, when they were interrupted - Brenda by a young airman who whisked her off in time to the music and Jane who found herself partnered with a young pilot called Billy Wilson. He was full of 'vim and vigour' (as she described later), with good rhythm and timing. They swirled about - ***slide, step, slide, step,*** trying to avoid cashing into the other couples on the dance floor.

In the far corner by the tables, Jane caught sight of the Brigadier and his wife and for a brief moment she thought of Richard Reynolds. He had stayed with them, before his move to the Mess. They smiled and nodded as each other as she waltzed by, but it dampened her mood.

She was still waiting for that one letter that would explain everything.

'That was marvellous!' announced the young airman, as the music began to fade. He was beaming from ear to ear. 'Thank you! We make a great team!'

'We really do.'

'Best waltz ever.'

She smiled and took a step back from his arms.

'It was lovely.'

'How about a bite to eat? They've laid on a fish and chip supper for the die hards – the ones that kept going to the end.'

'Well, that's definitely us.'

They stepped out into the fresh air; paper cones in hand filled to the top with salty chips and fish pieces.

It was dusk and it would soon be blackout.

'Can I see you again?' he asked enthusiastically, as they walked side by side. 'I've had a wonderful time.'

She stopped and smiled. 'Me too.'

'We could go to the picture house,' he continued. There's a show on at the Albany, *The man in Grey*. I believe it's marvellous.'

'I've heard it's good.' She hesitated. 'Listen Billy, I have had the most wonderful time tonight, really I have. It's just.....'

He looked at her. His enthusiasm had carried him away. Now, he could see that this chestnut haired lady looked a little sad.

'It's just that I have just come out of a little heartbreak.'

He nodded, knowing the bubble had burst and feeling somewhat despondent. 'Of course. It's no problem. Thanks for being my partner tonight and I'm sorry if I monopolised you!'

'I was happy to be monopolised. You're a wonderful dancer.'

His face creased into a smile. 'Goodbye my friend. See you around.'

They hugged and as they parted he added: 'Sing and dance when you're sad.'

She laughed. 'I will Billy. I will.'

She watched him as he turned off the path, eating his salty chips and singing the songs that still rang in his ears. She just needed time. Besides, she really needed to focus on herself for a while and on the task of finding her father.

***

Dr. Richard Reynolds was deep in thought. He had made

his way across the quadrangle from his college and was now walking, head down against the wind, along the towpath that bordered the riverbank.

Cambridge seemed deserted now and any students still studying were safely tucked away from the cold east winds and ongoing rain. It blew in squally sheets, bringing the fish to the top of the water. The tethered punts rocked empty, idle and a little green from lack of use.

The path forked and today he chose the shorter, more westerly route; walking purposefully, pale faced and head down, with his hands pushed deep inside his pockets.

His work at Cambridge was a comfort. In the day he didn't have to think, to brood, or to question. Instead he could focus, prioritise, test and re-test. The team were making good progress and had designed a number of significant mechanical improvements towards pilot safety.

Soon he would be returning to Mayfield to craft them into reality.

He was brought up sharp by a sudden shout and a squeal of brakes.

'**CAREFUL**!'

A young woman on a bicycle skidded to a halt.

'Look where you're going Mister!' I nearly fell in!'

'My apologies,' he muttered. 'I didn't see you.'

'Really! The young woman tutted and pushed her bike around him. He doffed his hat and shook himself into the present.

He stopped for a while, checking his watch and watching as she disappeared up the path, wobbling on her bike and muttering to herself.

He pulled up his collar. It was nearly five o'clock. He needed to get a move on or he would be late. He started to quicken his pace, the same old questions retuning:

Surely he had explained enough to her? Couldn't she see that the situation was complicated, that he was obligated? Would she not have done the same if the tables had been turned?

It was a bitter disappointment that his letters had been followed by radio silence. Surely he had meant more to her than that.

She certainly had meant a great deal to him.

.

Chapter Eighteen

It was August and still warm. The stronger patients at Uxbridge had been pushed out under the veranda and V was one of them.

A nurse, immaculate in her starched uniform, placed a jug of water on the table next to her. 'You have a visitor Ma'am,' she said, 'and it's time for your next round of tablets.'

The Sister plumped her cushions and V leaned forward, shakily pouring herself a glass of water.

Most of it spilt onto the floor.

'Damn it! I'm sorry.'

'Don't worry. You're getting better all the time.'

'I'll keep practising.'

'You must, I'm told you want to fly again.'

'I don't think so. I'm struggling to get used to the straps and my left arm has a will of its own.'

'Your skin will toughen up. You'll get used to it.'

'I doubt it.'

'Now, that's not the talk I expect from one of the few women who has actually been in the air. I don't believe for a second that you got to that point without some grit and determination!' The nurse tutted and shook her head. 'Enough of that now. I'll fetch your visitor.'

V pushed her head back against the cushions and shut her eyes. She heard the door open and then the tap of something ion the floor.

'Morning BH!'

The voice seemed very far away, but strangely familiar. She opened her eyes. The blurred vision had righted itself and now she was seeing everything as she had before.

'Lord! I mean *good morning* Ma'am.'

It was the captain; a halo of neatly brushed red hair framing her bird like face.

The young woman immediately attempted to get up.

'At ease officer. No need to stand on formality.'

Pops Hadley took off her hat and placed it on the table.

'Ma'am,' V fell back on her seat and mumbled to herself: 'Word travels fast.'

The captain smiled. This time her whole face seemed to crease with amusement. 'I see you still have that silver tongue of yours cadet. I would have come earlier, but I was waiting until I had some news. How long have you been here now?

V sighed. 'Six long weeks Ma'am.'

The captain drew up a chair, resting her cane on the floor.

'It's good to see you.' She paused. 'You had us all a bit worried back there.'

'Ma'am.' V rested her head back against the chair.

'You were lucky. It could so easily have gone up in flames.'

'So I've been told.'

'We're expecting you back up of course. Anything short of that would be a ruddy waste.'

V shut her eyes. 'Not possible,' she said, shaking her head.

'Now why do you say that?'

Suddenly, V felt irritated.

'Isn't obvious Ma'am. This arm is useless.'

'Well, that's not the voice of the cadet I used to know.'

'No - well she's changed.'

'Now listen here Bowes Hudson. Whilst it's true we haven't always see eye to eye, you were without doubt, a damned good pilot.'

'Yes, well those days are over.' V looked at the captain. 'I'm right-handed; how would I manage the controls?'

'That's why I'm here. I think I may be able to help you.' The captain looked at her, remembering their first encounter. Far better the slightly arrogant, but confident young woman she was then, than the frail and dismissive creature she was now.

'Now listen to me.' The captain pushed her chair a little closer.

'Ever wondered why I'm not flying?'

She turned round and picked up the hair from the back of her neck. There was a tangle of scars.

'Shot down by friendly fire. Anti-aircraft gun over

Southampton, poor visibility. I was mistaken for a stray. Burnt like that on my back and legs too.'

She tapped her left leg, 'and this.' She knocked through her tights. 'Buggered!'

'I did wonder. I'm sorry.'

'No need to be. There's a war on out there. A nightmare of a war. Every day there is a new space at the Mess table. We are the lucky ones.' She paused, then hesitated. 'You see I have regrets BH. I could have flown again. Other pilots have. I *could* have got back up there, BUT I lost it, lost the nerve. I'm not saying I don't enjoy what I do now, but I was trained to fly.'

'Ma'am you were badly injured. No one would have expected it.'

'No, they didn't. But I expected it of myself.'

'Well, I can understand that.'

'I admit that I didn't have the greatest impression of you when we first met. You were an arrogant young thing and you'd been playing with aircraft.' The captain picked up her cap from the table. 'But that wasn't the woman I saw by the end of that training. I saw a different character then; one who was brave, determined and focussed.'

'Perhaps.'

'No *perhaps* about it. I've talked to the doctors. We can get you back up on one or two specific planes if we produce an arm that will help you with the job. I've made some inquiries. They can make you a new arm; with four spring-loaded pins, like fingers, which will enable you to use the controls on the port side of the cockpit. The Hurricane might be a possibility then.'

'Is that really true?'

'Completely so. They've already got pilots back in the cockpit that way.'

V looked at her carefully. 'Okay. Well ...' She hesitated. 'I'll think about it.'

'That's the spirit. The captain's voice softened a little. 'Do you want to tell me what happened?'

V sighed wearily. 'I was trying to roll. I misjudged the speed, a wing tip hit the ground and it cartwheeled. Well, that's what I've been told. I don't remember much.' She paused, picking up her glass and shakily bringing it to her lips. 'It was a crazy thing to do. I suppose I'll get in trouble for it.'

'It's done now. Not much point in that. You just need to get better.'

'I was an idiot captain.'

'We've all been that at times - BH. We've all been that.'

***

The doctor took a step back and looked at the new arm in place. 'Good, now let's see how you get on with that.'

V moved her arm from her shoulder and felt the buckles against her skin. 'It feels strange Doc, but I guess I'll get used to it.'

'The main thing is to make sure you practice those everyday tasks, brushing your teeth, hair - that sort of thing.'

'And what about flying?'

'I think you can do it. You just need to build up some strength and coordination. The captain and I have discussed what's needed. This arm is your best chance.'

V took the doctor's advice. She started to use the gymnasium to build up her stamina. She also took long walks around the hospital grounds.

Slowly things started to become easier and she was grateful for that.

She was seeing out her last few weeks of convalescence when news started to filter through that the North African campaign had taken a turn; Rommel's troops being routed, and Tobruk taken. The hospital was told to get ready for casualties. New beds appeared and spare rooms cleared out. Suddenly, there was an influx of patients suffering from wounds, which had initially been treated by casualty stations at the front.

'How can I help?' she had asked when she heard of their coming.

'Sit with them, read to them, help them write letters home,' the nurse said, watching V wash her hair. 'You're getting better at that.'

'Thank you,' she said. She was starting to feel more interested in keeping herself 'well groomed.'

The nurse laughed. 'When you talk like that it reminds me of a dandy brush and a whinnying horse!'

She was glad the officer was feeling better.

The hospital soon filed up and there were no spare beds left on any of the wards. It was hard to sleep at night with the crying and shouting out. Young sailors and soldiers flooded the corridors and V volunteered to give up her bed.

'Where would you sleep officer?' The doctor admonished, 'and no you're not quite ready for discharge yet.'

'But I feel so useless and guilty.'

'Guilty?'

'My injury being self-inflicted.'

'Look,' he said. 'Self-pity is pointless. You had an accident. It happens. Get over it and do something useful.'

'Right Doctor.'

'Any comfort you can offer will be more than useful.' Then he added a little more gently:

'Scrub your hands and get down to see where you can be useful.'

***

'Nurse, nurse read to me!'

The young soldier held out a small notebook, filled with poems and pastings.

'I'm just called V. Just V.' She smiled and sat next to him. She could see he was missing a leg.

'This is a beautiful book. Did you do these sketches yourself. They're simply marvellous.'

She opened the pages carefully. There were about a dozen or so pencil sketches of the desert and his comrades.

He didn't answer. His head was bandaged, and she could only see his eyes; they were those of a boy.

'There's a poem in there.' He said weakly: '*To a rose in bloom*... It's my mother's favourite.'

V started to read and at the end of every heart wrenching line she looked to see his eyes slowly shutting and his hand gripping hers.

By the time she had finished he was asleep, and her eyes were wet with tears.

Chapter Nineteen

The pilot pointed the nose of the plane in the direction of the Maintenance Unit. This was his last drop off for the day and they were flying over new terrain. It was thickly wooded and not far from the coast; the grey sea clearly visible in the distance.

'This is a new MU for me. Not been to this one before.' The pilot scoured the landscape for somewhere safe to land.

'Me neither. It seems they're becoming more isolated,' observed Jane, checking her maps.

'Dispersal's the only way. Keep your eyes out for a suitable landing area.'

Jane rifled through her collection of papers.

'According to the map, it's in that forested area down there!'

'Ok. Well it looks pretty dense in that direction, but we'll give it a try. This should be interesting.'

The pilot started to lower the plane, circling widely over a canopy of trees; the throaty sound of the engine grumbling in the silence of the sky.

'Is there a sign of anything?'

Jane scanned the landscape below. She could see a trail of smoke, presumably from a train running on some tracks in the distance, but very little else. The forest seemed to stretch for miles.

'Not a thing!'

'Ah wait,' the pilot had spotted something, 'what's that over there – two o'clock?'

'Yes, you're right, there is something over there. It looks like a clearing. Yep, that must be it!'

'OK. This will be tight! Hold on!'

The pilot approached the clearing cautiously. There was very little room for manoeuvre. The Avro brushed the tops of the trees as it came into land, bumping to a stop.

'Phew! That was close,' said Jane letting out a sigh of relief. ' I don't think I could have landed so well in such a tight spot.'

'Of course you could! Anyway, remember you have to fly out of it!

Jane laughed, unbuckling her belt. 'That's true! By the way, there's a party later. Verona Bowes Hudson's back.'

'I heard.' The pilot smiled. 'And perhaps with a little less bravado!'

'We'll see. At least she is on the mend now.'

'And hopefully, not likely to take any chances again!'

'You don't know V!' remarked Jane laughing and jumping down from the aircraft. She waited for a while as he manoeuvred around and took off again, skimming the tops of the trees.

Taking off will be difficult she thought as she spotted what looked to be a further small clearing through the forest. It looked to be a wide track and likely the runway. She started along it until she came to a pile of wet ropes on the ground. She had reached the perimeter of the unit. Trees had been pulled down to make way for it. Once completed, they had cut the ropes and the trees had snapped back to provide camouflage for the structure.

A large metal hanger loomed up in front of her.

'Mosquito collection!' She called out into the dark, damp space inside.

A man appeared blinking into the daylight, wiping his oily hands on rags.

'Morning, Ma'am.' He took the chit and looked at her. 'You found us then!'

'Yes, eventually! It was very hard to find, but I guess that's the idea. You know, I think I've see you before.'

'Probably,' he nodded. 'I've been all over!

'Perhaps at Southampton?'

'That's right. But they moved the factory from there. Target you see. Now we're here and out in the sticks. We can barely find it ourselves! All sorts of places being used for MUs now: old workshops, garages, barns, sheds. Cup of tea?'

'That would be wonderful. Thanks.' She followed him inside.

There was a small pan of water, boiling on a stove, the steam evaporating into the abyss of the giant workshop.

'It's weak I'm afraid. Rations are thin.'

'It's tea. That's all that matters,' she said, taking the tin mug.

'Good.' He smiled, leaning back against a wall, his face creasing into the smudges of oil across his cheeks.

'What's it like where you are?'

'Madness!' she said, sipping the tea. 'Every day is crazy! You wake up and can't imagine what you'll be doing next. How about you?'

'Same,' he said. 'Subscription age has been reduced again and so many of the lads that used to help have disappeared. We have a lot more work now; meanwhile the war is spreading all over.'

'It's relentless,' agreed Jane, emptying her cup.

The mechanic pointed over to a green-grey twin-engined, shoulder-winged plane. 'That's yours. We'll get her out for you. Here are the pilot's notes.'

'Thanks.' She zipped up her flying jacket and followed the Mosquito's tail out into the sunshine.

***

Phyll was shattered. She had completed her last drop off and was keen to get back. *How much longer would it take?* The taxi flight seemed to have landed at every airstrip between Lyneham and Broadlands. She was uncomfortable too; squashed between spare parts, food, newspapers, and medical supplies.

Resting was out of the question; Brenda was waiting for her when the Avro landed. She was out breath and in a hurry.

'V's on her way back and earlier than expected. She'll be here in ten minutes! Reception party has been shifted to the station.'

'Wow ok. What do you need?'

'Just yourself now, we've already dragooned as many as we could.'

They got there just in the nick of time. The welcome party was already assembled. Banners and bunting lined the platform and a group had gathered along the bank to the side of it.

A loud cheer erupted at the sound of the engine as it came around the bend; its brakes screeching loudly; the spare steam wafting through the air as it approached the platform.

The whistle sounded and inside the engine, the fireman opened the box, the glow of the fire lighting up his weather worn face. Inside the compartments, the passengers started to gather their belongings, V spotting the waiting crowd with some apprehension.

Truthfully, she would have rather slipped in unnoticed. The confident young woman had largely disappeared alongside her hospital stay. Endless recuperation had prompted much reflection and now she didn't feel quite so sure of herself. Not that a stranger would have been to tell as V was good at hiding things.

V spotted the captain, small and bird like, her red hair

curling around the edges of her cap. She had a lot to thank her for and she must have made a special trip to Broadlands for this occasion. She had been relentless in her determination to get V back up again. Her encouragement and support enabled her to see that life could resume as well as it had and that there was also every chance that she could fly again. Something that meant a great deal to her.

She checked her hand mirror and adjusted her hat as the train jolted to a stop. *Here goes*, she thought, standing up to pull a small case from the racks above.

The guard began to open the doors, doffing his cap as he reached her.

'Need any assistance Ma'am?'

'I'm perfectly capable.' She replied a little testily. 'But good of you to offer,' she added, as she stepped down from the carriage towards the far end of the platform.

The guard chuckled to himself as he helped a woman with a pram further on down. He had heard about the famous 'V'. Her reputation preceded her.

Outside the cheering and whistling was in full flow and she could now see all her friends; Jane, Phyll, Maria, and Brenda. It was just Hattie who was missing, still recuperating on leave. The sight of them, filled her with emotion, a little unusual, given that she was unruffled by most situations. *Now pull yourself together. You can do this* she told herself as she battled with both the joy and trepidation at the reality of returning.

The captain stepped forward and with an intonation of triumph, saluted the young woman.

'Welcome back Cadet.'

V stood to attention. 'Thank you, Ma'am,' and then drawing in a deep breath, added quietly, 'thank you for everything.'

The captain nodded. 'It's a pleasure. Glad you've come back to us,' she said, motioning to shake hands.

V froze. She had forgotten that this familiar greeting, would be offered at some point. For once, she wished that the crowds could melt away; but then she would not be showing courage and *courage* meant a lot. It had been her brother's favourite word, especially when he was teaching her to fly. What would he have said about this situation?

What are you doing Verona! Don't be a ninny. You've practiced the same movement in other ways and many time over!

This poignant reminder bought her sharply to her senses and straightening herself up, she took the captain's hand.

There was a huge cheer from the crowd and feeling an element of relief, she turned to them and waved adding:

'Thank you and how delicious!'

Her friends put their arms about her and hugged her with Phyll laughing and exclaiming: 'Now that really does sound like the old V!'

'Ok, cadet,' interrupted the captain once there was a lull in the excitement. 'The next item on the agenda is a trip to Hanger 8.'

'Car's ready now Ma'am,' observed Phyll indicating towards the lane outside the ticket office.

There were a few more handshakes with the assembled crowd and then V was off, being driven along the lanes, sandwiched, between Jane and Phyll, with the captain in front next to the driver.

'Now close your eyes before we get inside' said Phyll, when they reached their destination; a heavily camouflaged hanger, hidden along the perimeter fence.

Soon, they were all assembled; V with her eyes shut tight and Jane and Phyll on either side of her, amongst the familiar smell of oil and rubber.

The captain switched her torch on. 'You can look now.' She flashed her torch across side of an aircraft. 'The Hurricane! A great little plane, enclosed cockpit, retractable undercarriage and…'

V gasped as the captain flashed her light across the nose of the aircraft revealing an inscription:

Semper pergendum sine timor

'Remember any schoolgirl Latin BH?'

V read; her voice breaking. 'Move forwards?'

'***Always*** move forwards ***without fear*** cadet .*Always move forwards*.'

For once V was simply lost for words. 'Thank you captain,' she said with conviction.

'It's a pleasure.' The captain nodded. 'This aircraft will help you get airborne again. I am absolutely sure of it.'

Chapter Twenty

Phyll was sitting on a suitcase, trying to snap the clips together.

'Bother! How come I managed to fit everything in before?''

'Here let me help you. It'll shut if I sit on the case.'

Jane obligingly did the deed and Phyll closed it with two satisfactory clicks.

'Excellent. It looks like we are both pretty much set to go!'

They both had leave. Phyll was heading back to Cardiff, whilst Jane was on her way back to her mother's, heralded by a promising letter sent from the ministry:

October 23rd 1943

Dear Mrs Harrison,

I would like to express the squadron's sympathy for not writing to you sooner with details of your husband, Squadron Leader Gerald P Harrison's disappearance.

We can now confirm that the aircraft in which he was flying was lost over or near Reims and despite efforts to the contrary, we have been unable to establish what has happened to him.

You may be aware that in some cases aircrew reported missing are eventually reported as being prisoners of war.

Once again please accept our sympathy and let us hope that we may have some more constructive and positive news soon.

Yours sincerely,

H. P Johnson Wing Commander

'I have a good feeling!' she proclaimed excitedly, showing Phyll the letter.

'It's certainly more information than you've ever had and Reims narrows it down. You just need some intel.'

'I know, but how?'

Phyll shook her head. 'To be honest lovely, I've no idea. Everybody's keeping 'mum' these days. The only people who probably could help are some of the boys in the squadrons, word of mouth-that type of thing.'

'So could Eddie find anything out?'

Phyll's expression clouded over. 'Well you know I would ask him, *if* I knew where he was, but I've heard nothing - not for weeks now.'

'No news is good news Phyll. You know that.'

'That's what I have to keep telling myself.'

'Didn't the Kenley boys say that his squadron might be overseas? Perhaps Eddie's in France too?'

'I know, but really he could be anywhere; even over the Atlantic'

Jane looked crestfallen.

'Look I'll see what I can do. Maybe the boys do know more now. I'll put some feelers out.'

Jane hugged her friend. 'Thank you, Phyll. I'd really appreciate it.'

***

Reconnaissance had its dangers and life on the island of Malta was becoming increasingly grim. Endless sorties, loss of friends, constant bombardment, it was all wearing down the most resilient of spirits.

Eddie Edwards felt quite ill on it.

He knew Phyll would be worried, but it was almost impossible to send out personal messages now.

How could it have got to this?

He wrote anyway; a letter full of cryptic messages, disguised in a note about a fictional dog. He delivered it to HQ alongside a bundle of still wet photographs and hoped for the best.

By some miracle it did find its way across the sea. The post room had picked it up. It was marked *Broadlands* and managed to filter through.

Having arrived at the RAF station, it was redirected immediately to the family's home in Cardiff, the address which Phyll had given on signing up. It came, hand delivered by the sub postmistress and was there on the table waiting for Phyll when she finally arrived back home for leave.

'Thank goodness I gave this address. I didn't want anything coming to an empty flat..' Phyll began to open it with a knot in her stomach and began to read.

'Is everything alright love?' her father asked, bringing her a cup of tea.

'I think so Dad. Listen to this. It's a minefield of cryptic clues.'

Aristotle sounds wonderful. He'll make a companion for little Spitz.

'What on earth does that mean?'

Her father sat down in his favourite armchair, sucked on his pipe and tried to make sense of it. 'Spitz? That's a little dog isn't it?'

'I think so. So why Spitz? Why Aristotle?'

'Perhaps it's a **variety** of Spitz? Her mother suggested. 'Try the encyclopaedia.' She dug out a large heavy book from underneath a side table.

Phyll located 'S' and followed her finger down the page.

Spitz *A type of domestic dog characterised by long thick often white fur. Examples: Huskies, Maltese, Pomeranian...'*

Her father, puffed for a moment, the tobacco smoke filling the area around his armchair.

Then he smiled. 'Maltese…Malta?'

'Yes maybe. That could be it!'

'There's every possibility. Malta is heavily under siege at the moment.'

'But what about *Aristotle*?' Phyll bit her lip.

'Well, you've got me there.' Then he smiled and added gently. 'But you can ask him when you see him.'

'I'm just relieved he's ok.' Phyll leaned back in the chair and stroked the little tabby cat that had just jumped onto he lap. The fire crackled in the grate and she began to relax.

'Write back to him lovely,' suggested her mother, 'address it to HQ? There's a chance he'll get it.'

'I will mother. Besides, I need to ask him about something really important. ' I need to ask hm about a missing….,' then she stopped short. *Damn it! This is what the war had done to her, done to all of them.*

Her mother came over and kissed her on the head. 'Keep it to yourself dear. Tell us when it's all over.'

***

Muriel Harrison had not told Jane how ill she was; her daughter had enough to think about. She couldn't say when the cough appeared, but appear it did, with a shortness of breath and a vice like headache.

She wrote to her daughter, being careful with her words:

Don't be alarmed dear. Dr Cunningham's says it's just a touch of bronchitis and really nothing to worry about. Miss Collins next door has been most kind. She has been bringing soup and making those lovely raspberry buns that don't need an egg.

She phoned the Farm Vet and explained that she was sorry to let him down but was feeling rather unwell. This had been difficult to do; he would be shorthanded yet again. She was a farmer's daughter and knew how hard this would be. She would even miss the slog of farm visits in winter. They had been a welcome relief from the constant worrying about her husband.

Now she had stopped working and those worries were flooding back.

She took herself to bed with a cup of warm water and a teaspoon of honey.

Things were more serious by the time Jane arrived home. She found the curtains shut and her mother soaked through - exhausted with the effort of breathing. Immediately she called Dr Cunningham.

'It's bronchial pneumonia.'

'Poor mother. Shouldn't she be in hospital?'

'She's probably better at home, provided there's someone to take care of her; there's a bout of influenza going around. I've prescribed some medicine, but someone needs to make sure that she takes it regularly.'

'I'm on leave for a week,' said Jane taking the bottle from him.

'Then she'll definitely be better off here. Give her rest and lots of fluids. I'll pop back in a few days to see how she is. Oh, and damp air raid shelters won't help. The more you can keep her out of those the better.'

'I'll do my best.'

Jane waved him off, by which time her mother was asleep again, hair soaked and cheeks flushed with fever. She squeezed a flannel and held it to her brow. She was glad she had come home. It felt like old times, but at the same time it did not. In truth, she felt a little numb; the distinction between life in the ATA and home seemed strange and so different now. She kissed her mother's cheek and went downstairs to stoke the stove, pushing the wood around the grate.

***

It was true that all the friends were feeling the difference between civilian life and the ATA, but for different reasons. This was especially so for V who had spent weeks recuperating, via Uxbridge and was now back in the full swing of training with her new prosthetic.

'How have you been lovely?' asked Phyll on her return from Cardiff. 'Hope the captain is going easy on you!'

'She's been relentless! Though I am feeling a little better I must say.'

Phyll hugged her, 'You look a million times better! She just wants to see you making progress that's all.'

'I know and in all honesty, it's probably working. I've been pacing myself in a dual controller, just to get the feel of things. I can't count the times she's had the Squadron Leader take me up. She wants me back in the Hurricane tomorrow!'

'That's brilliant.'

'Nerve-racking actually!'

'Now come on, where's that VBH grit!'

'A little bit further down the road I think.' V smiled ruefully. 'But I'm up for giving it a try. I have to, the captain's invested in me now, even though she's barking commands all the way from Mayfield! By the way, bad news about Jane.'

'Yes, it really is. She's been through the mill; what with her father, the mystery of the illusive Dr. Reynolds and now her mother being ill.'

'Well we'll write to her and keep her up to date with things. Are you straight back out tomorrow?'

'I am.'

'Then you won't see my attempt to get the Hurri up!'

'You'll be wonderful, lovely. I know you will.'

'Hopefully, with good weather and luck on my side!'

***

V had spent a fitful night and when dawn broke she was up at the break of it, pulling on her flying suit and making her way out and onto the perimeter track that led to the hangers.

The Hurricane was waiting for her, pushed out the previous evening and now resting under some camouflage nets.

First problem: how would she get those off on her own?

'Hello! Her voice echoed around the empty space in the hanger behind. Anyone about?'

'Can I help Ma'am?' A bleary-eyed boy (for he seemed no more than a youngster), emerged from the shadows of the hanger. He was wiping oil off his hands. He had been on the night shift and was about to knock off.

V felt more than a little relieved. 'That would be most helpful.'

He nodded, blinking as he stepped out into the early morning light. He noted her stiff arm and the mechanical hand protruding from her jacket cuffs.

'It's no bother Ma'am. I've got a couple of hooks for that net..'

He disappeared for a moment, returning with a couple of poles with hooks on either end.

'Here,' she nodded, 'pass one over.'

'Are you sure Ma'am? Honestly, I can drag it off in a jiffy.'

She smiled. 'Absolutely sure. I've got to fly the beast. I think I can manage.'

He nodded passing her one of the poles and watched as she grabbed it shakily with her left hand. 'Ready?'

'Ready!' They pulled and it slid smoothly off onto the tarmac.

'Excellent! Problem solved! Now for the next one.'

'Ma'am?'

'Getting in! I used pull myself onto the wing .'

'Ladder Ma'am?'

V considered this, but decided it was now or never.

'No I think I will try myself first.'

'Yes Ma'am.' The boy began to bundle away the netting.

'Let me know when you're ready Ma'am; I'll take the chocs out.'

'Will do.'

Locating the stirrup-shaped step from the lower fuselage she grabbed the hand hold to haul herself up. This required a few goes. She didn't want to use her new arm in this way and her left arm was much weaker than the right one used to be. Eventually and through sheer determination she managed it, pulling herself over the sill and punching the air triumphantly as she did do.

This would take some getting used to.

She looked about the cockpit and felt a knot in her stomach. Everything would need to be considered with only one functioning arm. The aluminium one was stiff and inflexible.

Now everything seemed like a tangle of levers and handles.

She carried out her pre-set checks and pressed the starter button. The propeller started to turn, and there was the familiar growl of the Merlin engine.

OK Verona.. This is it. Steady yourself.

She gave the thumbs up. 'Chocks away!'

The boy ran to remove the wedges, waving her off. What a story he had to tell! Everyone had heard about the famous Cadet and her aircraft with the personalised inscription.

Always move forward. V was thinking about those very words as she taxied her aircraft to start of the runway. She grasped for the brake lever and remembered the captain's words*: a hand with four spring loaded pins should enable you to use the controls on the port side of the cockpit.* She tried to give the brake lever a squeeze.

It wouldn't budge.

'Come on!' She pulled harder. Suddenly, it released itself.

Gently, she moved the lever to raise the undercarriage, reducing the propeller speed for the climb.

She was airborne.

'My God, I've damned well done it!'

Chapter Twenty One

Phyll's letter to Eddie had arrived via a filter room in Malta. Operations were communicating directly with radar stations around the islands and information and post was being received from various places, including the naval station at Auberge de Castile and from overseas.

Her cryptic note was just one of many notes picked up or sent through. It lay there amongst an eclectic assortment of both personal and military communication.

Phyll had thought hard about the letter she needed to send to Eddie. She had to carefully construct something that might give Eddie some clues as to where Jane's father had been reported missing. In the end she settled for something obtuse and just prayed he would be able to read between the lines:

***Harrison's** still missing.* She had written:

*We're so worried because he's such an old cat. Maybe he's been **picked up** by some kind family who have taken him in. **Reims** is missing his brother so much! He has taken to sitting on the fence all day. I know he is looking out for him I've placed a notice on the parish notice board and I've described his **left blue eye with its splash of brown.** I've put up posters everywhere. On a brighter note, the carpenter says he will be able to repair the door,* *even if it is in the old style! Thankfully, door repairs are classified as an essential. He's measured it at **5 foot 10 inches**. No wonder you bang your head each time you come through!*

It wasn't difficult to piece the clues together and he wasted no time in broadcasting a description:

Squadron Leader G Harrison believed missing over Reims. August 1940 (Air Striking Force). Description: around 47 years of age, 5ft 10, blue eyes; left eye has a splash of brown.

Not the most detailed description but it would have to do.

For a while there was nothing but silence; but then snippets of information began to filter through. There was a pilot of that description, but he wasn't in France, he was in the Pyrenees. He had been picked up by the Comet Line, an underground movement in both France and Belgium and who were helping to organise the escape of allied Airmen.

He may well be who Harrison was looking for?

It could be him. It was worth looking into. He messaged his contact.

'Let me know as soon as you hear anything else.'

Somehow, the search for the missing pilot made him feel closer to his wife and there was comfort in that.

***

Gerald Harrison looked about the kitchen, with its blackened range and giant scrubbed table. The longer he stayed, the more he worried about Claudette. The farm was situated on a hillside and had a view of a valley through which ran a road between two towns. It was one of Claudette's duties to keep her other compatriots informed of all troop movements up and down the valley and she had been on watch that day.

Twice now he had come close to being discovered when soldiers had been sent out to check whether the farm could provide any supplies. He would hear her footsteps approaching, running frantically over the stones in the courtyard.

'Hurry Monsieur. Hide!'

That was his cue as she bundled him behind a secret partition in her wardrobe, suffocating and dark, soon to be followed by an agonising wait as soldiers shouted and banged around the room in front of him.

He was mightily afraid for her.

'Don't be, Monsieur Gerald,' she had said one night while he stirred the *cassoulet* in the pot. 'I have nothing to lose. I stay here, keep the farm going, turn the soil, feed the goats and chickens and wait for news of my parents.'

'You have everything to lose. It is very dangerous my dear,' he spoke in a fatherly way, as he would do to Jane. 'To stay out of it might be better. To keep yourself safe, for when they return?'

They spoke in this way, almost in riddles, skirting around

the likelihood that her parents might never return.

'As I say Monsieur, I have nothing to lose.'

Later, after the fire had died down he used a knife to cut into the lining of his jacket. 'I have a few francs. Take them Claudette. We were given some in case of an eventuality such as this.'

'Merci,' she said stuffing the notes inside her apron pocket. She was about to poke the fire when she stopped and in hushed, anxious tones whispered:

'Did you hear that?'

The sound of footsteps was approaching from outside.

Claudette immediately tightened her grip on the poker.

'*Qui vient?*' Her voice shook as they stared unblinking at each other.

She started to raise the iron above her head, her hands trembling as she lifted it into the dusty air of the fading fire.

There was no answer, but the footsteps stopped. There was a rustling sound and a piece of paper appeared, pushed under the gap between the door and the flagged floor.

Claudette breathed a sigh of relief and lowered the weapon.

'It is fine as you say in England. We are safe!'

'Are you sure.' The pilot hauled himself up to standing. 'Please let me check.'

'No need. I know what it is.'

She placed the poker back down near the fire and scooped the paper off the floor.

'The signal has come.' She looked across at the pilot. He looked tired and not as well as she would have liked.

But there was no choice.

'We are to catch the first train from Dijon to Avignon tomorrow morning.'

Gerald nodded vigorously. He could barely believe it.

'What can I do to help?'

She looked up, her face looking tired and drawn; she had practised this sequence many times before

'Check you have all your papers and remember your story.' She tucked the letter into her apron pocket and walked back towards him. 'Remember Monsieur, you are Basile Martinez, my uncle from Avignon. You have been staying with me for a while.' She put her fingers to her lips, 'and most importantly, you cannot speak. You have been traumatised by a bombing raid, during which you lost your wife.'

He nodded 'Yes, yes.. I will remember.'

She nodded, satisfied that he understood.

'Get a good night's sleep now. We have a long day ahead tomorrow.'

He nodded and began to walk stiffly towards her; his stick tapping on the cold, flagged floor.

'Thank you Claudette. I don't know how to repay you.'

But she was already disappearing up the stairs. The time had come to move on - for both of them.

***

Claudette woke early with the shadows of night dissolving. Outside, she could see dawn, the first blush of sun as it rose above the horizon.

Today, as she did every day, she made wishes. A wish on the lavender fields bathed tangerine in the growing light; a wish on the blue grey sky filling with streaks of silver and gold; a wish to keep her parents safe and a wish to keep this man safe. This man who was somebody's husband and somebody's father.

She shivered, gathered herself up and pulled on a dress over her night clothes.

'Wake up Monsieur Gerald. Time for us to go now!'

She cut slices of bread and cheese, wrapping them firmly in muslin.

'Here we can eat on the way. We have about an hour's walk to the station. Will you be able to manage?'

'Yes of course. You watch me.' He smiled, trying to sound more confident than he really felt.

'Good! Then we are ready.' She passed him a small suitcase of gentleman's clothes. 'For you.'

He nodded. The reality of returning home was starting to sink in. He wanted it so much, yet there was a long journey ahead and he was not strong or completely recovered. She had explained what he would be up against; mountains to climb, rivers to cross, tunnels, tracks and safe houses to find.

He was under no illusions how difficult this would be.

'You first Uncle Basile!' She smiled as she waved him through the doorway and into the chill of the cold morning air.

'Merci Claudette. I repeat - how shall I ever repay you?'

She smiled as she pulled the door shut behind them, adding: 'I think Monsieur you are starting to sound like 'a cracked gramophone!'

He laughed, an action that always sliced through his anxiety. 'The perfect idiom!'

'Yes and taught to me by the last airman who stayed here. I am learning all my English from my unexpected guests!'

They set off, exiting through the farm gate and onto the long straight road. The chill of early light soon starting to evaporate as the sun climbed higher in the sky.

The journey was a difficult one for Gerald Harrison. A doctor examining him would have concluded that he had crushed some vertebrae, alongside his chest injury. This resulted in a painful and teeth gritting walk, with many stops along the way.

They arrived at the station later than expected. This meant that the platform was already busy; a situation Claudette had been hoping to avoid.

'We must limit out conversations,' she whispered, waving to a farmer, with chickens in a basket. He screwed his eyes against the sun and looked at her companion with curiosity.

'That man knows my family. We must do nothing to attract attention.'

The train arrived, steaming to a stop. There was a rapid exchange of people through the doors, and much commotion and door banging.

'We should find a carriage near to the end of the train,' she whispered, 'look for an empty one.'

They were in luck. The passengers on the busy platform seemed to have disappeared, melting away into the rest of the train.

'Keep your head down and keep reading,' she whispered, her gloved hands clutching a book. 'Remember, you are a scholar, Monsieur Basile Martinez. My very learned Uncle Basile.'

'Arts or Sciences?' he whispered as the doors banged shut and the whistle blew.

She did not answer. She knew he was using humour to calm his nerves, but she was frustrated that he had spoken at all.

'*It is dangerous to speak*,' she had warned him.

She sighed and started to open the pages in her book.

The train began to chug and jolt. Steam crept in through the ill-fitting windows, alongside a strong smell of coal and smoke.

For a while they sat in the rocking carriage, half reading, half alert to any approaching footsteps. Their papers would be checked. It was not something that either one of them was looking forward to.

The airman's eyes began to close, lulled by the warmth of the carriage and the movement on the tracks.

The rocking motion soon changed into a vision of his Spitfire as it lurched in the sky, and he was falling again as he had through many dreams, down, down into the tree tops. But this time they didn't catch him and he kept falling and falling and fall….

A voice pierced his dreams. Good, he had been picked up by friendly faces!'

'Ihre Papiere bitte!'

He awoke with a start.

The young soldier standing over him did not appear to have a friendly face at all.

Gerald Harrison came immediately to his sense. Claudette was fumbling in her bag; there was a second soldier standing over her too.

'Beeil dich! Schnell!'

'Oui, je les ai ici,' she said rummaging away, her hands trembling.

*Oh Claudette, you **do** know how much you have to lose!* He felt overwhelmed by the courage of this woman. They **had** to pass these checks. He reached inside his jacket and heard the click of a gun pointing straight at him.

Slowly he raised his left hand and reached for his papers with the other. It was hard to breath.

The soldier snatched his ID and examined it closely, turning it this way and that in his hand.

'You. Why are you here? You are from Avignon?' He spoke in French.

Harrison kept his eyes down, his body rigid.

Claudette spoke up again. 'I'm sorry Messieurs. He is unable to speak. He is suffering from shock. He lost his family in a raid and has been staying with me. I'm his niece. Look we have a note from his doctor.'

Only the pilot could hear the raised, brittle tone in her voice.

The soldier looked at his compatriot. The other shrugged his shoulders and tapped his watch. There appeared to be some argument between them. The soldier examining Claudette's ID wanted breakfast. He was hungry and was in no mood to argue the toss.

The young shoulder threw back the airman's ID.

'Very well,' he said at last, moving on down the corridor.

Chapter Twenty Two

Muriel Harrison was recovering. The fever passed and she began to regain strength, helped enormously by the care she had received from her daughter who had managed to extend her leave, realising that she needed more help than originally envisaged.

Jane was a little concerned about how her mother might cope once she returned as it was proving difficult to find anyone who might be hired to give a little extra help until she was completely strong again. For a start there was the difficulty of where the cottage was located. The lane outside was so full of pothole's that it was hard to traverse either by car, bicycle, or horse.

On top of that was the problem of hired help. Anyone not called up was now preoccupied with efforts on the home front. Villages, towns and cities were running on full throttle (as their neighbour Miss Collins liked to call it). If the people were not busy planting vegetables and knitting blankets for 'the boys,' then they were stepping forward as volunteers for the Home Guard or other such vital roles.

Two weeks had passed since Jane's arrival back home and it was a dark and snowy January morning. She had been to fetch duck eggs for breakfast from the farm further down the lane and was now trudging back up, having found two large pale blue ones nestled in a box by the gate.

She found her mother downstairs when she returned. She had a towel and kettle in hand and was pouring water into a teapot.

Come and warm yourself by the fire dear. I've got it going for us.'

Jane stamped her boots on the doormat and the snow slid off them, melting onto the floor.

'Mother, you know you should be tucked up in bed. Please don't come down the stairs on your own. I need to help you do that.' Jane took off her damp scarf and put her hand out for the kettle.

'Here *you* sit by the fire. I'll finish that.'

Her mother nodded. 'Ok dear,' she said, sitting down and watching her daughter pour hot water over the leaves. 'Listen Jane, I want you to go back now. I can't ask you to spend any more time nursing me.'

Jane shook her head, stirring the tea. 'No mother, you are still not strong.'

'Really, I'm fine. I can cook a little *and* walk to the end of the lane.'

'Well, I shall worry about you.'

'Then we shall worry about each other,' she said, beginning to pour the tea.

'Well, let's see what Dr Cunningham says. We can make a decision then.'

'I am sure he will be perfectly fine about it. Maybe we could ask Miss Collins if we might share her niece for a while? Perhaps, she would be happy to do a little shopping for me.'

'That is a possibility.'

'Then that's settled then. I'll ask her.'

Jane took a sip of tea and changed the subject: 'Weather report has been updated. I heard it on the radio; snow clearing, clear skies over London tonight and we know what that could mean.'

Her mother frowned. 'Yes, another restless night for us all.'

'Exactly, bad news for the city and everywhere else on their way back .'

'Cargo drops before the channel!'

'I'll head off into town tomorrow mother, to see what else we can scrounge off the ration book. We don't have too much in. Clear skies are forecast for the rest of the week.'

Her mother agreed and as predicted the sirens broke out not long after blackout. They could be heard all over the countryside in the still of the evening.

'Come on dear.' Her mouther shouted above the wail. 'We must get to the shelter. I'm well enough to go outside now.'

'No mother! Doctor Cunningham said that the damp's not good for you.'

'Well we can't stay here. There's no protection at all if something drops.'

'We've been under the table, on and off for the last few

weeks, another night's not going to make any difference.' Jane guided her mother to the mattress which they had left under the large, scrubbed table.'

Mrs Harrison's breath rattled as Jane wrapped her in a blanket. 'Listen to you mother! You're in no state to go outside. Come on, let's make ourselves comfortable.'

Just as they were settling down their neighbour Miss Colline appeared with head around the door.

'Room for one more?'

'Of course, come in! Here, let me help you.'

'Thank you Jane dear. Your mother and I have spent every night together since the air raids began. I'm not breaking with tradition! Here take this. I've brought a tot of whisky for our nerves!'

They needed the strong spirits. The railway line, at the bottom of the hill, had a mobile gun on it and the noise was horrendous.

The night was spent fitfully, punctuated by the sound of whistles and explosions. Aircraft were dumping bombs before it hit the Chanel and dawn broke to an eery silence.

The three women crawled stiffly out from under their make shift shelter. Muriel Harrison switched on the radio; there were reports that Rye had been targeted down near the harbour and other areas 'further out' had suffered from bombs and bullets, an unexploded one currently sitting on the railway line not far from the centre of town.

'I'll go down there after breakfast,' said Jane, stoking

the fire in the range and putting a pan of water on to boil. 'I'm sure they'll need all the help they can get.'

By the time Jane did reach the town, work was already under way; made doubly difficult by the freezing cold temperatures, so early in the day.

The damage was clear to see. Shops had been reduced to rubble and glass and debris was everywhere. Neighbours shovelled in silence, shifting debris into wheelbarrows, sifting out what could and couldn't be saved.

I must get back to Broadlands, she thought, her eyes looking skywards. *It is where I am supposed to be. I should be flying again..*

Jane joined in, wheeling barrows to and from the back of a cart. At lunchtime, the baker whose ovens could still be lit, brought out hot potatoes; one of the few items that were not rationed. They were most welcome and on the back of them Jane stayed for most of the day,

It was nearly dark by the time she found herself walking back up the lane towards home.

'Is everything ok dear?' her mother asked, as she came in through the door. 'You look exhausted. Here, give me your coat and put this blanket around you.'

'It's a terrible mess mother. Old Percy's shop is flattened, which might make getting groceries a difficult for a while. In fact, there is quite a lot of damage all along the main street.'

Her mother ladled some soup from a pan. 'They were obviously getting rid on way back from London.'

'Almost certainly and goodness knows what's happened there.'

'Come and sit down and have something to eat and I'll put the radio back on. By the way there was a call for you earlier. It was your Mayfield friend Phyllis Edwards.'

'Phyll? That's lovely. Did she say why she'd called? I'm afraid no news is good news these days.'

Her mother passed her a slice of bread and butter.

'I'm sure it's nothing to worry about, she said she would ring back later.'

Jane woke with a start. It was nine o'clock. The heat of the fire had overcome her and she had fallen into a fitful dream. London was ablaze and V and Phyll were calling to her across the rubble.

In her waking consciousness she became aware that the telephone was ringing. It's shrill bell causing it to vibrate on the small table on which it was perched.

Jane rubbed her eyes and shook herself awake.

'Is that you Phyll?' She could barely get the words out.

'Hello Jane.'

It was not the voice of her friend.

'Who'd speaking please?'

'Jane it's Richard…Richard Reynolds.'

'Oh God!' She caught her breath.

'I wanted to catch up - to see how you are.'

'How I am?'

'Yes. I'm sorry I didn't mean to alarm you. I just wanted to apologise – to explain.'

She was lost for words.

'Jane?'

'Yes, I'm still here.'

'I didn't mean to shock you.'

There was another pause before she said stiffly:

'Yes, well you have.' Why are you calling? It's been so long. How did you get my number?'

'Your friend, Phyllis Edwards. She gave it to me.'

'Phyll?' She felt a little sick. 'What do you mean?'

'I bumped into her at Mayfield. She was on a stop over.'

'I don't understand.'

'I wrote to you Jane, every week for months, letters to explain, letters to help you see.'

'What are you talking about Richard. I have not received any letters.'

She felt confused and a little irritated. His voice seemed a million miles away. She had forced him to belong to the past. So much had happened since then and he felt a world away.

'Look Richard, I wish you well, with life, work, everything, but let's just leave things as they are. I have not had any letters from you. I don't know why you would make such things up. Now please leave me alone and we can both just get on with our lives.'

She replaced the receiver and when she did so, she found that her hands were shaking.

'Is everything alright dear?' Her mother called from upstairs and then as she came down added: 'I didn't want to disturb you. How's Phyll?'

'It wasn't Phyll mother. It was Richard.'

'Richard?'

The phone rang again.

They looked at each other. 'That is probably Phyll now. Would you like me to tell her you'll ring back tomorrow?'

'No, it's ok.' Jane head was spinning. 'I need to talk to her.'

She picked up the phone and a familiar lilt came over the wires.

'Hello lovely!'

'Phyll.'

'It's great to hear you. The girls send their love; we're missing you like crazy!' Phyll carried on quickly. She knew her friend would find her news difficult. 'Now listen lovely, I'm sorry to ring so late and I want you take a big breath....'

'You saw Richard?'

'Yes...yes I did! Oh bother! How did you know?'

'He's just rung me. You gave him my home phone number.'

'I did, but damn it, I wanted to speak to you first.'

'Why did you give him my number Phyll? You know how I feel about things!'

'I do and that's why I gave him it. Listen. Grab a seat. There are things you need to know because it may change how you feel.'

'How I feel?'

Phyll hurried on. 'I did see him Janey. It was last Friday. I was delivering a Spit to Mayfield. He was coming out of a hanger; he had been working on something. I didn't recognise him at first. He looked pale - thin. Not well at all.'

'Well, I am sorry to hear that of course. But that's his problem. Phyll.'

'I know….. I know. **But** there was a reason why the woman was in his room that day. Look, she wasn't his fancy piece if that's what you're thinking. She was the lover of a young boy that had been killed in his squadron.'

'I don't understand.'

'Apparently, the young man had been in his squadron and had been shot down. He said that he had spoken to you about it before?'

Suddenly it came back to her. It was this incident that had prompted him to stop flying and move back to Cambridge, to further research into aircraft safety.

'Ok.' she said slowly, trying to gather her thoughts. 'But Phyll, she called him 'Dicky'. There was a familiarity there.'

'Maybe there was, but for completely innocent reasons. You see, she was expecting the young man's baby.'

'Oh my word.'

'Yes, expecting and all alone with a family who wouldn't have anything to do with her. They weren't married you see.'

'But that's terrible. I don't understand it.'

'Absolutely and there's more. The young woman was ill, or rather she became ill. She was desperate and turned to Richard. There was limited time left and a small child to make arrangements for. She asked him if he would care of the child.'

'Oh Phyll. There's so much to take in. Why didn't he explain? Why didn't he tell me.'

'He tried to - many times. He wrote every week for months.'

Jane shook her head. 'He said he had, but I never received those letters.' Tears stung her eyes. 'What on earth happened to them. Where did they go?'

'He said he sent them to your home address. He didn't want them opened at the station.'

'No of course not. Well as far as I know they've not arrived. I'll ask mother, but she would have said.'

'It does seem strange.' Phyll gathered her thoughts. Her friend had so much to take in.

***

Jane was packing. News had come through that the Ferry Pool were returning to Mayfield and she was preparing to join them. Any extra support for her mother, would be provided through an arrangement with the niece of their neighbour, Miss Collins, who would be able to runs some errands alongside those that she did for her aunt.

The mystery of Richard's missing letters were solved by virtue of the very same Miss Collins, who lived in the cottage a little further down the lane. The reserve postman had posted the first letter to her home by mistake. A brief conversation by the garden gate soon revealed this error, with Miss Collins kindly offering to take it up to the Harrison's place next time she went.

Except she forgot.

Her letterbox, a small cast iron affair set deep into a stone wall by her gate, soon filled up with more letters, each with the same methodical handwriting.

Miss Collins did not have many relatives and received very little post. Consequently, the letters accumulated unnoticed and *'what with the air raids and everything I simply forgot to check.'* By the time she eventually came round to doing it, she was faced with half a dozen, damp letters, all addressed in running ink.

The letters spelt the story as set out by Phyll. Jane read them all and her heart fell into a million pieces. She discovered that he had kept his word and when the young lady had passed away, he had taken the child, a boy, under his care. He was just one year old. During the day he was cared for by a woman in the town with a family of her own, but in the evenings and weekends he cared for the child as well as any father would.

Immediately, Jane sat down to write her own letter; the ink flowing across the page, slanting with the haste in which she felt she must write it.

***

'He's on his way home!' Phyll was jubilant. 'Eddie Edwards is coming home!'

Her husband's telegram had been short and sweet:

Kings Cross STOP Saturday 22nd STOP 4pm. STOP

A raft of tired heads lifted from newspapers, letter writing and other off duty activities.

'That's wonderful news darling!' V lit a cigarette and took a long and pleasurable draw. She was resting in a chair, with her shoes kicked off and legs tucked under her.

'When's he back?'

'Saturday. I'm to meet him at Kings Cross.'

'Well that's wonderful news. I hear it's been bloody in the Med. He'll be glad to get away for a while.'

Phyll arranged some leave and took the train to London the following morning. She rode the northern line to their flat in High Barnet, half expecting it to be flattened, but it was still standing, albeit, amongst the debris of the night bombing raids.

Her footsteps echoed on the empty, dusty stairs. It seemed eerily quiet, compared to the days when music would play through gramophones and radios would play the latest tunes.

Once inside, she opened the windows and turned back the covers on the furniture. The place smelt musty and damp; hardly surprising, for they had only spent a couple of nights there before being catapulted into the theatre of war.

She looked at her watch. Only two more hours until Eddie's train would roll into London. She kicked off her shoes and lay on their bed, listening to the sound of buses in the street below. She felt so tired; there was just no let-up for any of them. This is now how she felt anytime she was off duty; undoubtedly caused by early starts and late night finishes. Her eyes stated to shut and she began to doze. She dreamt of home in Wales, and the purple heathered mountain at the back of *Gwaelod Y Garth* reaching up to the clouds. Eddie was there flying through them. Onwards he flew towards Mayfield. until he reached the battered airstrip at sunset. In her dream she was running towards him, but he was unable to land; a plume of smoke billowing from the engine, flames licking the cockpit.

  'Eddie!' She woke with a start, breathing rapidly; a band of sweat across her brow.

For a while she sat on the side of the with her head down. *Another one of those dreams.* She stood up and splashed some water from the kitchen tap onto her face. Patting her face dry and looking in the mirror, she realised how thin she had become. Gone were those rosy cheeks of life before the war, flushed with the air of the hills and valleys. Now her face was pale and wan, with eyes circled by shadows. She wasn't alone. All her friends were like this now. Their energy burned up by the relentless attack on the nerves, their flying becoming increasingly treacherous.

Phyll took a deep breath and began to brush her hair into shape. She had bought her best hat and would not wear uniform. For once, she decided against it. She didn't care if she got into trouble. This was Eddie she was meeting and she wanted him to see her amongst the crowds.

King's Cross was packed. It was full of soldiers, civilians and children who were being endlessly evacuated or returning. Phyll threaded her way through them, her heart beating with excitement. She noted that a part of it was cordoned off due to bomb damage and one of the lines was shut.

There was only one train due in at four. Phyll hovered outside the platform hoping for a glimpse of her husband through the crowds.

He saw her first. She was wearing her hat of cornflower blue; a present he had bought her on their engagement. They ran into each other's arms and he lifted her off the ground, twirling her round and holding her tightly.

'Oh Eddie. You're safe! Thank God!'

'I love you Phyllis Edwards!' he hugged her tight and they kissed each other, patting and touching each other as if hardly believing they were next to each other again.

'Where have you been?' she whispered in his ear.

'In some far flung places that's for sure!' he winked at her and squeezed her tight. 'Let's just say that the sun shone in the Med. Oh it's good to see you Mrs Edwards.'

'Let's get out of here Eddie,' she said taking his hand.

'Listen,' he said, letting go of her hand and stepping back a little. When he did so, she noticed he was turning and nodding behind him. 'I'm not alone love. I've brought someone with me.'

She hadn't noticed the man, standing quietly behind, with a small brown suitcase in his hand. He wore a Homburg hat and an ill-fitting suit. His face was pale and drawn, but he was smiling and looked very familiar.

Her heart skipped a beat. It was a smile she recognised.

The man held out a hand and she took it, holding it tightly and shaking it vigorously.

'Welcome home Squadron Leader Harrison.'

Chapter Twenty Three

Muriel Harrison had always believed her husband would return. Of course, many pilots had 'come down' and not survived, but it was the ministry's word 'missing' that had given her cause for hope. She clung to this word. Missing was *not* the same word as dead. She had even taken to looking up the word in the dictionary; a small, battered book that her husband had loved to pour over when doing his crosswords:

Missing*: (a person) absent from a place and of unknown whereabouts*

There it was in black and white! To presume death would have meant giving up hope and she had *never* been ready to do that.

In fact this was so much the case, that she was strangely unperturbed, when her daughter took the call from her Mayfield friend - Phyllis Edwards.

It was the weekend before her daughter was due to return to duty. Jane's suitcase was already leaning against the back door. She had packed early in anticipation.

Muriel Harrison had gone to bed early. Her neighbour's niece would be over the following day and she wanted to get a good night's sleep in preparation. Of course she would be glad of the help, but really she was sure she would be able to manage things now.

Jane was on her way upstairs when the phone rang. At

First there was nothing but strange clicks and tones. Then Miss Collins could be heard on the line: 'Hello, hello, hello!'.

Crossed lines were casing a problem again.

The operator tried again:

I have a connection for a Miss Jane Harrison.

'Yes, that's me!'

'Sorry dear I thought it was a call for me!'

'That's ok. Have a lovely evening Violet!'

'You too dear!.'

Click and the line cleared.

I have a Mrs Edwards on the line. Will you accept the call?

She relaxed a little, grateful it was her friend and not somebody else with a 'bad news' call.

'Yes that's fine. Please put her through.'

A familiar voice came over the wires. 'Wonderful news lovely! Are you sitting down?'

Jane smiled, a surge of excitement passed through her. 'Wonderful news is always good!'

'Rather *delicious* as V would call it!'

'Oh my goodness, now you have me on tenterhooks!'

'Ok, brace yourself!'

Jane caught her breath.

'Eddie has found your feathered friend!'

Jane sat down, confused. 'My feathered friend?'

'Yes, his wings were damaged, but he's on the road to recovery.'

Jane's heart jumped. Suddenly, she knew *exactly* what her friend was talking about.

'Eddie found him and he's very proud of himself I must say!'

Jane instinctively put her hand to her mouth, smothering a cry. But the tears in her eyes said it all.

'I can't believe it!' she said choking over the words. 'Thank you. Thank you *so* much - both of you .'

'You're welcome ! We'll arrange for him to be sent over tomorrow. He'll need a lot of tender loving care. Good night and sleep tight!'

Jane dropped the receiver and for a while it swung on its chord until eventually, she picked it up and place it back down again. Then she hid her face in her hands until a strange noise erupted in her chest, consuming her with a sobbing so loud, that Miss Collins could hear it next door and came rushing over to see whatever was the matter.

***

Gerald Harrison had shrunk into exhaustion. He was feeling every bump of the rattling jeep. The thought of home was overwhelming him. He had waited so long for this moment.

How would he ever be able to repay all those who had helped him along the way? Those who had clothed, fed and sheltered them, at great personal risk to themselves. Those who had helped him with the treacherous and long journey through France and onwards. Indeed where would he have been without the Edwards too. Eddie who had single handedly picked him up and flown him back to Kenley and Phyll, who had passed on essential messages, ones that were needed to raise the questions necessary as to his whereabouts.

Now he was home and he could barely remember how long he had been away.

He recognised Rye emerging from the fields as the light started to fade. His driver was complaining, mostly about blackouts and headlights. They were behind schedule. A road block along resulted in a long detour, during which they had double backed upon themselves more than once. By the time they reached the town, dusk was beginning to fall.

'Sorry mate,' the driver said, pulling up outside the butchers shop; four fat wheels bouncing to a grinding halt.

'I can't take you any further. I have to get back to my sister's before blackout and I'm not sure I'll even make that now. I'll have to drop you here if that's ok.'

The pilot nodded, thanking the man as he pulled his bag from the seat beside him. 'Thanks for the lift. It was much appreciated.'

'No trouble.' The driver nodded thinking: *I wonder who he is, all dressed in civvies. Seems an educated man but could equally be an educated bad'un. On second thoughts, he looks a bit shelf shocked, maybe he has seen a bit of action. Nobody tells you anything these days!*

'Be careful on that road mate,' he added, 'and sorry again that I can't take you further.'

Gerald Harrison waited for the truck to pull away before crossing the road. Many of the lights were out already. A short walk and he was back amongst the crisscross of narrow streets that made up the bulk of the town. He weaved his way through them, trying to remember a shortcut that could take a pedestrian straight to a major junction; one which would set him on the right road.

Eventually, he came upon a familiar fork in the road; one direction took you back via a route into town, the other led eventually to the sea. Pulling up his collar and with his head down he set off along the narrow harbour road; the chill of winter whipping around him, the last of the light diminishing rapidly.

After a mile or so, the road started to melt into a single track, leading to the coastal byway.

He had reached home

He stopped momentarily by the gate, or rather the gate posts, for the ornate metal defences were gone, commandeered for smelting down. For a while, he listened to the wind as it whipped around the trees in the little garden. They were close to the sea here and the trunks were twisted and bent; the bark gnarly and splintered with the salty air.

He noticed the old apple tree, lying on its side. It was not a surprise; it was hard to keep anything rooted here. The fallen tree prompted a memory; a small child playing and laughing on a swing amongst its branches. That little girl was now grown up, but he had no knowledge of what had happened to her since his capture, or indeed that she had joined the ATA.

The chill penetrated the pilot's bones, and he shook himself into the present. Exhaustion, emotion and the relief at being home began to overwhelm him. He took the final weary steps through the gap where the gates once hung and down the well-trodden path.

'He's here mother!' his daughter cried and like a small child she flung open the door and wrapped her arms around him so tight that he nearly fell over.

'Gerald,' Muriel Harrison was almost lost for words. 'Oh my goodness! You're home, you're safe!' Husband and wife hugged each other, lost for a moment in the world of the familiar. 'Come in,' she said taking his arm, 'let's get you out of the cold.'

Inside, they brightened the oil lamps, wrapped him in a blanket and plied him with hot, sweet tea.

He was almost too exhausted to talk; too weak to move, so they tucked him into a makeshift bed and stoked the fire. It roared warm and comforting and they sat with him until late into the night and until he fell asleep. Then they left him, shutting the door softly behind him, and holding hands with joy as they climbed the box stairs to bed.

Gerald Harrison awoke with a start. He thought he could see a red tin roof; blue sky shining through the cracks. For one moment, he imagined he was back in the barn, hearing Claudette as she clattered down below with the goat's milk pail.

Except he was not. He was at home again, lying on a bed by the fire, the flames of which, Jane had built up in the early hours of the morning.

Jane bought him a cup of tea and he started to come round. Propped up with pillows he began to talk. Slowly at first, faltering over the beginning, as though stuck in that place; but as the morning moved on the story started to unravel.

He had been flying over Reims. His squadron had been sent there following the seizure of an airfield. There was suspicion that the Luftwaffe were using it as a maintenance and repair base. They had reached their destination but were ambushed almost immediately.

'What happened father?'

'The Luftwaffe had scrambled a squadron. One minute I had been weaving at speed through the sky, the next the aircraft came to a juddering halt, hit by a stream of bullets.'

Jane quickly rested her hand on his arm. 'Father, you can tell us as much or as little as you like.'

'It's ok, my dear. I was one of the lucky ones. Out of my squadron, only five of the twelve airmen returned.'

His daughter hugged him. It was almost impossible to believe he had made it.

'The battery of fire, tipped the Hurricane onto its nose and I was looking straight down, thousands of feet below.'

His wife gasped. 'On its nose?' She repeated incredulously

'Yes, and with no way of pulling out of the vertical.'

'My goodness Gerald, what a nightmare!'

'It was, but you see I was lucky. By some almighty stroke of luck I managed to bail out. I don't remember too much after that, except when I awoke I found that I had been rescued, helped by a group of brave souls who had saved me.'

'Who were they Gerald? They saved your life!'

'They were a group. Let's just say that. I was taken to the house of one of them,. A girl not much older than you Jane,' he said. 'I had bullets in my chest and legs, but she managed to dig them out. She looked after me until my fever was gone and my wounds healed. She was so brave. On more than one occasion the army passed by, but she kept her nerve. It must have taken every ounce of strength not to show how afraid she really was.'

Muriel Harrison clasped her hands to her chest. 'She saved you Gerald. This girl saved your life! What was her name?'

'Her name was Claudette. Her parents had been part of…' he stopped short, aware that to say anything else would be folly.

How could he explain? *Careless talk costs lives.* This warning had been drummed into him so many times. How could he share it all, even with those he loved the most?

Jane smiled and hugged him. 'No need to say.'

But he so badly wished that he could. How she was part of *La Resistance*, a collection of French movements fighting against the Occupation and how dangerous their work was. He wanted to tell them how she was carrying on her parents work after they had 'disappeared'. That they had to plan in secret with meetings held under the cover of darkness and in which contacts, strategy, papers, and routes out of France had been discussed.

Then there were the many who helped him along the way, who clothed, fed and hid him, at great risk to themselves. These people helped him escape through France and Belgium - all the way to the Pyrenees, where treacherous weather and his own frailty nearly killed him.

How could he explain the terror of some of those nights, holed up in tunnels with the soldiers ever present and on the lookout. Or the relief when he finally made it over the Bidasoa river and into Spain.

'Many kind people helped me escape,' he said eventually, 'and I needed their help for the journey was long. I crossed France and finally into Spain. From there I was taken by a free Norwegian boat to Gibraltar, where Eddie Edwards, who had been given a tip off, was able to meet me.'

'All those kind people who helped you,' said his wife shaking her head. 'There's a special place in heaven for them.'

'If you still believe in that my dear. The things I've seen...' He sighed, a long deep and weary sigh.

'And what of Claudette?' asked Jane, squeezing his hand. 'Did you hear from her again?'

'I'm afraid not. But, after this war ends - and it *will* end. We will find her, yes? All of us. We will find her and thank her.'

Jane smiled. 'We will do that. We will find her again.'

Epilogue

The engine thundered down the track as the firemen shovelled the coal in as quickly as they could.

Steam billowed past Jane's window as it sped past hedgerows, villages, rivers, churches and streams. For a while she considered her reflection in the window. She needed the sun, the green grass of the aerodrome, the rays streaming through the clouds.

Soon she was closing her eyes; lulled by the warmth and the movement of the carriage. Slowly her book dropped down to her lap.

Her mind drifted back to the blitz and to James Ford, with his whole life ahead of him; to young Tommy Mitchell, now mended and back at Broadlands, to V and to how she had fought herself back into the sky, to Richard Reynolds who had put duty before himself, to her mother who had never given up and to her father whose life had been saved by the courage of many, but particularly that of a young woman, not known by any other name except Claudette.

The train leaned around and bend and Jane was awakened by the banging of doors and a shout from the guard.

'NEXT STOP-MAYFIELD!'

He poked his head into the carriage.

'REMEMBER TO TAKE ALL PROPERTY WITH YOU!'

Sleepily she stood up, stretched and pulled her bags down from the luggage rack, catching sight of herself in the scratched and mottled mirror. She felt different somehow, perhaps a little delicate; so much had happened since she had first arrived at Mayfield. In addition, the anticipation and excitement of seeing Richad was almost too much to bear. She reached for the soft toy she had bought, a little dog with a tartan collar; a present for the little boy.

A shriek of brakes and the train began to slow down. Outside the station master's cat stretched out his soft white paws, unperturbed by the rattle of metal and the hiss of steam.

Phyll pulled down her suitcase and straightened her jacket. 'This is such a strange feeling,' she said handing V her paper.

'Because we're back where we started, or back in Topsy Turvey Cottage? Oh, leave the paper darling; someone else can read it. The news coming in is truly awful; makes one even more determined to stop this madness.'

'I second that,' said Phyll holding onto her hat as the train juddered to a stop. 'Here's to peace and freedom. For everybody, wherever they may be.'

The three women piled their cases onto the platform. There was a smell of smoke, coal and the scent of spring.

'Where's the truck to pick us up?' V looked around. 'You did give them our ETA Phyll?'

'Oops. I might have forgotten! Here I can manage yours too.'

'Certainly not! V grabbed her bags in irritation.

Phyll shook her head. 'You're so stubborn sometimes!'

'Come on,' said Jane, watching V stride off. 'We have to sign in by two and we don't want to miss seeing the others, especially Hattie.'

'Of course, I'd forgotten that she's back today. Marvellous!'

'You're starting to sound like V,' laughed Jane picking up her bags.

The lane from the station soon merged onto a wider road. They waited as a fleet of RAF supply jeeps passed by; once painted blue but now a camouflage green.

'Wait more traffic!' called Phyll as they were about to cross again. A figure on a motorbike was approaching; the low grumbling engine becoming louder until it caught up with them and stopped.

The man grinned, his wheels resting on the tarmac. 'Crikey! What a small world! Got your dancing shoes with you!'

It was the young airman, from the Summer Ball at Broadlands.

Jane laughed. 'Hello Billy! It's good to see you again!'

He nodded and opened his throttle. 'Likewise! On your way to Mayfield too? Seems like we're all being sent here!' He began to push himself off, then paused. 'Listen, that offer of a date still stands – if you're still free?'

She smiled. 'You know Billy, I think I might be taken now!'

'Just my luck!' he rolled his eyes laughing.

'Any room for a passenger?' V stepped forward. 'It seems a shame to waste that back seat!'

'Hey if it's not the famous Bowes Hudson. You are quite the talk of the station!'

'Of course, darling,' she said with her usual flourish. 'Famous or infamous-take your pick!'

The young man laughed. 'I'll be the talk of the town if I give you a lift back! Hop on!'

'Marvellous! Let me just arrange things!' she said squeezing her bags onto her lap. 'Just one too many, be a darling Phyll and take the small one for me?'

'Yes M'am! Toss it here!' Phyll caught her small suitcase laughing. 'That's right, happy to be your stooge!'

With that they were off, with the engine roaring and V's hair unravelling as the trail of smoke followed them to the end of the lane.

'Now that's the Verona we know so well!' Phyll laughed, beginning to walk a little faster.

'Hey, wait for me!' Jane caught up. 'This all feels very strange.'

'Strange?'

'Oh you know, here we are right back where we started.'

'*Déjà Vu?*'

'Exactly. It's almost like we've been caught in a whirlwind and one that's not going to stop.'

'Yes, but it has to, one way or another. At some point it must end and then we can all return to the lives we knew.'

Phyll stopped for a moment and dumped her bags on the ground. 'One minute's rest! How come my bags are twice as heavy as when we left. We weren't away that long!'

'Long enough!'

'Hey look Janey! Eyes upwards. Three o'clock!' They stopped and shaded their eyes. 'It's our old friend, Tiger Moth. I can see a splash of yellow.'

'So it is - must be the new ones coming up. We really have come full circle!'

Her friend shrugged; picturing the pilot's view from amongst the fragile clouds of spring. 'Or have we just carried on, just kept moving forwards?'

Phyll picked up her bags again. 'You know when I was at school we had a motto: *What stands in the way becomes the way.*'

Jane laughed. 'That sounds deep. What's it about?'

'I think, my friend, it's about resilience and moving forwards.'

'Well we've seen plenty of that!' Jane grabbed her friend's arm. 'Truck coming!'

They leaned back into the hedge as another convoy of truck passed them.

'Let's get our papers ready.' Phyll began to rummage. 'Ah here they are!' she said smiling and holding them up triumphantly. 'Ready Jane Harrison?'

Jane held her own papers aloft, 'Ready Phyllis Edwards. Let's pray this is really our last move.'

'Amen to that! To Mayfield, to Broadlands, to *any* aerodrome! Let this war end soon.'

Now enjoy!

'A blast of a Blog!'

Jane's Diary

Share in Jane's friendships, passions, challenges and triumphs!

Blog @ Janesdiary.co.uk

Follow Jane's story as she writes about her experiences at Mayfield and Broadlands and about life in 1940's Britain.

Jane's Diary

POSTSCRIPT

Notes from Author

Historical context of *Jane*

Whilst **Jane** is a piece of fictions, it nevertheless attempts to place the story within the historical context of the work undertaken by the Air Transport Auxiliary (ATA) during World War Two.

The Air Transport Auxiliary (ATA) was founded at the outbreak of war, in 1939. It was a civilian organization which carried out the ferrying of aircraft between factories, maintenance units and front-line squadrons.

Women were able to join following lobbying by Pauline Gower, who herself was an accomplished pilot. These pilots were nicknamed "Attagirls". The first eight women pilots were accepted into service as No 5 Ferry Pilots Pool on 1st January 1940. The pilots in Mayfield Six belong to fictional Ferry Pool 6a

In total around 10% of ATA pilots were women and they attracted a great deal of interest from the press. This can be seen in Chapter 15, when a housemaid spots Jane Harrison in her flying suit:

'Mary, would you believe it!' whispered the younger girl excitedly. 'I think she was one of those 'ATTA' girls. You know-like the ones in your magazine!'

The ATA developed its own training programme and pilots could progress from light, single-engined aircraft to more complicated and powerful aircraft. At the start of the novel, the group are flying the Tiger Moth a small lightweight plane, but by the end they have moved onto more complex and heavier aircraft.

Training was usually caried out in stages; the first being *Class 1*. Pilots gained experience by undertaking ferrying work of any and all aircraft in that class before moving on to the next stage. V, Jane, Phyll, Maria, Hattie and Brenda all move onto Class 2's when they move to Broadlands. In total there were six stages in which a pilot could progress.

The ATA flew thousands of aircraft around the country and were essential in freeing up RAF pilots for combat. Often they flew with very few navigational instruments and of course at the mercy of the British weather!

After the war ended, most pilots returned to civilian life, but for many their lives were changed forever by the experience.

The ATA motto was: Aetheris Avidi 'Eager for the Air', with the unofficial motto being affectionately known as: *Anything To Anywhere.*

The units were disbanded at the end of the war in 1945.